DISTRACTION
TRAVERS AND PALUMBO
BOOK 2

PETER MULRANEY

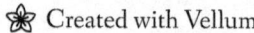 Created with Vellum

In memory of Asher

CHAPTER 1

D<small>R</small> S<small>AM</small> T<small>AYLOR</small> had spent a long Monday doing what he could to keep the desperately ill Covid patients under his care alive. Exhausted, he exited the hospital at the end of his shift looking forward to a good night's sleep, before having to come back and do it all again.

In the fog of his tiredness, the eighteen kilometre drive to his home in High Street, Stirling, seemed to take forever. In reality, it took him a little over thirty minutes, like it did most nights.

Sam pulled into the driveway of the house, nestled among a forest of towering eucalyptus trees on the outskirts of Stirling, one of the older settlements in the hills east of Adelaide. They'd bought the place for its secluded location three years ago when he'd secured his position at Flinders, the main hospital servicing the southern suburbs. He pressed the button on the remote resting in the well of the centre console and waited for the roller door to lift, before driving into the double garage at the front of the house.

As he listened to the roller door closing, Sam sensed that something wasn't quite right. His wife's car was parked in its usual spot but the door leading into the house was open, and the interior of the house through the open doorway was in darkness. Sarah always shut that door - they had a four-year old daughter.

Sam walked into the hallway and flicked on the lights. 'Ella! Daddy's home!'

He waited for Ella to come running into his arms as she did most nights when he announced his arrival home from work. There was no sound of movement from within the house.

'Sarah?'

Silence. What were they up to? Were they planning some sort of surprise for him? It wouldn't be the first time they'd done something unexpected to welcome him home from a stress filled day at work.

Sam walked down the corridor turning on lights and peering into rooms as he went, half expecting them to appear from their hiding place. There was no sign of them, apart from the backpack Ella took with her to kindergarten sitting on the kitchen bench.

Standing in the living area, he checked his phone for messages in case he'd missed one from Sarah. Nothing. He called her number and heard what sounded like her phone ringing from somewhere outside. They must be hiding out on the alfresco. He could almost see the frown forming on Sarah's face, knowing she'd be disappointed he'd resorted to ringing her phone, instead of waiting for them to spring their surprise.

He turned on the lights that illuminated the alfresco dining area at the rear of the house and stepped outside through the sliding glass door, expecting them to shout: 'Surprise!' But there was no shouting. There was only an involuntary gasp when he spotted Sarah, sprawled on her back next to the garden bed with a startled look on her face.

Instinctively, Sam bent to check Sarah's body for a pulse, knowing he wasn't going to find one. He'd seen enough dead bodies to know she wasn't alive the moment he'd spotted her lying on the paving stones. Her neck was cold to his touch. He pulled his hand away, sank to his knees and screamed. After the day he'd had fighting to save lives, coming home to this was just too much to bear.

After a few moments lost in absolute anguish, Sam got to his feet slowly and looked around. What in God's name had happened? Had she tripped and hit her head? It didn't make sense. Sarah was athletic. She had a great sense of balance. She didn't go around tripping over herself.

Sam realised he might be going into shock. He couldn't let himself do that. He took a couple of deep breaths and told himself to stay calm. He had to find Ella. Where was she? She must be frightened. She would have been at home alone for hours, going by the temperature of Sarah's body.

'Ella! It's Daddy! Where are you?'

No response. Not even a sniffle.

He ran into the darkness of the yard, beyond the reach of the light illuminating the alfresco, calling her name. He crashed into the wheelbarrow he'd left in the garden on the weekend and tumbled into the remains of their summer vegetables.

He dusted himself off and went inside to get the torch he kept in the laundry, then returned and searched the yard calling her name until his voice was hoarse. There was no sign of her. Perhaps she had wandered off into the forest surrounding the house in an attempt to get help from one of the neighbours.

Sam didn't know what to think. Sarah was dead and Ella was nowhere to be found. He leant against a tree, fighting back tears of desperation.

Realising he'd need help if he was to find Ella, he pulled out his phone and called his father-in-law: the Police Commissioner.

CHAPTER 2

Two DAYS after the news of Sarah Taylor's death and the search for her missing daughter had become headline news across the nation, Detective Sergeant Pat Travers returned to work after a mild case of Covid. As soon as he'd sat at his desk, intending to log on and work through his inbox, he was summoned into Detective Inspector Smith's office.

'Have a seat, Pat,' said Inspector Smith. 'How are you feeling?'

'Right as rain, sir. It'll take more than bloody Covid to kill me.'

'That's the spirit.' Inspector Smith shuffled the papers on his desk until he found the one he wanted. 'You hear about the Commissioner's daughter?'

'Pretty hard not to,' said Pat. 'Any news on his grand-daughter?'

'Still missing, I'm afraid.'

Shit, thought Pat. Two days out in this heat, that couldn't be good. 'Who's leading the investigation?'

'Uniform are conducting the search and DCI Roberts is heading up the murder investigation,' said Inspector Smith, passing Pat the sheet of paper he'd retrieved from his desk-top. 'He's asked for you and Palumbo to be assigned to the investigation as soon as you returned from leave.'

Pat glanced at the piece of paper Inspector Smith had given him. He hadn't worked with Max Roberts since 2016, when he'd taken leave on the death of his wife, Pam . 'Why? I would have thought DCI Roberts has more than enough talent at his disposal.'

'This Omicron variant's been through the place, Pat. You aren't the only one it's hit, meaning DCI Roberts is short staffed. Besides, I understand the Commissioner wants you on the team.

'Oh,' said Pat, wondering why the Commissioner thought he had anything special to add to the investigation.

'Don't let it go to your head, Pat. He probably only wants a calm head in that team,' said Inspector Smith, smiling. 'Have you heard from Palumbo?'

'She'll be out of isolation tomorrow.'

'Good.' Inspector Smith leant back in his chair. 'DCI Roberts has set up shop on the fifth. He's expecting you at nine.'

'Right, sir. Guess I'd better go and see him, then.'

Pat took the stairs up to the fifth. It was only two flights and he knew he needed the exercise. Max Roberts had been his boss when he'd been just plain DI Roberts. Pat wondered if the extra responsibilities of being a DCI had curtailed Max's exuberance and his tendency to go with his gut feelings, instead of where the evidence suggested they should look. Hopefully, he'd get to report to one of

Max's underlings and not have to contend with the man himself.

'Ah, Travers,' said DCI Roberts, holding out his hand and then letting it drop by his side, as if he'd remembered they weren't supposed to be doing that. 'It's been a while. How are you? Heard you had the Covid. Man, I had it something shocking before they got the bloody vaccines rolled out. Sit down.'

Max hadn't lost any weight since Pat had last seen him but he'd lost most of his hair. 'I was lucky,' said Pat, sitting on the seat in front of the DCI's desk. 'Got away with a headache and just feeling sleepy for a week.'

'Must be the luck of the Irish, Travers. I was so bloody crook I thought I was gonna die. Ended up spending a week in Flinders but they brought me back from the brink. And, would you believe it, I was treated by the husband of our victim.'

'Small world,' said Pat.

'You can say that again. Wasn't expecting to meet him again under these circumstances, poor bastard.'

'Me neither. I was at their wedding.'

'Maybe that's why the Commissioner wants you on this case,' said DCI Roberts.

More likely he wants me to keep you on the straight and narrow, thought Pat. 'Could be,' he heard himself say instead. 'Anyway, it's been a couple of days, what do we know?'

'Not much,' said DCI Roberts. 'I'll send you the crime scene report. See what you can make of it.'

'Are we sure it's murder?'

'Pathologist thinks so. I'll send you his initial report as well.'

'Who will I be reporting to?'

DCI Roberts rested his arms on his desktop. 'I want you and Palumbo to report to me. I've got Derek Ryan. You remember him? He's a DI now. He'll run the incident room and organise the troops. I want you to review everything before we make any final decisions. Your job is to make sure we follow the evidence in case I get carried away. We can't afford to fuck this up, Travers. This is the Commissioner's daughter we're talking about.'

'What about the girl?'

'Not looking good, I'm afraid. Initially, we thought she'd just wandered off, so we searched the woodland around the house and door-knocked the neighbourhood. That was before Dr Taylor calmed down and had a good look around the house with the crime scene boys and girls. Now it appears she was taken by whoever killed her mother, since the good doctor is saying the child's car seat is missing from his wife's car and he thinks some of her clothes and toys are gone. '

'I guess we'll be hearing from her kidnapper, then,' said Pat, hoping she hadn't been taken by someone intent on hurting her.

'Yeah, let's hope it's someone with a ransom demand,' said DCI Roberts, 'and not some sicko who likes to abuse little girls.'

'Guess we'd better canvas both possibilities until we know for sure,' said Pat, not wanting to think about that particular outcome.

'I've got Derek looking at who might be a person of interest. Now, get out of my office and get yourself up to speed on the reports. Oh, and there will be a briefing out there,' said DCI Roberts, waving his right arm in the general direction of the incident room, 'at four. Best if you work down on the third and turn up for briefings. Don't want you being distracted, Travers.'

***

Pat logged on to his computer and opened the link to the case folder on the share drive that DCI Roberts had sent him. He located the sub-folder holding the crime scene files and started reading.

According to the report there was no sign of a forced entry, which suggested to Pat the victim had either known her killer or opened a door to him. It was too early to tell if any of the fingerprints lifted from the house belonged to her killer, that was something he'd have to follow up with the crime scene investigators. One item that caught his attention was the mention of dried drops of a liquid, possibly perspiration, which the investigators had detected on the upholstery of the rear seat of the victim's car next to where the child's car seat had been secured.

Pat sat back and thought about what that might tell them. He opened the pathologist's report and scanned it for the time of death. The initial estimate was late afternoon, somewhere between four and six pm.

Pat returned his attention to the details in the crime scene report. The victim's car had been parked in the garage. He opened an image of the property taken from the street. It revealed the house was a modern residence with a corrugated iron roof. If its construction was similar to most recently built dwellings, the garage would be a brick veneer structure with minimal insulation. It had been hot on Monday. The daytime temperature had reached thirty seven. Even at Stirling, up in the hills behind the city where the daytime temperatures were often several degrees lower than those recorded in Adelaide, the late afternoon temperature would still have been in the thirties. There was a reasonable chance, thought Pat, that those spots of perspiration belonged to the person who had taken the car seat out of the victim's car.

Pat knew sweat in itself held no DNA, but he was aware that any skin cells embedded in it certainly would. He also knew that people shed skin cells all the time, and made a note in his notebook to find out what the analysis of those drops of perspiration revealed. It might not identify their killer, unless he was already known to them, but it would provide a way of linking a suspect to the crime scene if they ever had a suspect to take a swab from.

According to the crime scene investigators, the tracks left on the carpet in the house suggested there had been at least two intruders and they'd worn something, probably plastic bags, over their footwear. That detail made Pat think they were dealing with people who had put some thought into what they were doing.

Pat wondered why they'd gone to the trouble of taking clothes and toys belonging to the child they'd abducted. That didn't read like the behaviour of someone obsessed with his own sexual gratification. It sounded more like the actions of someone intending to hold the child for a period of time and wanting to keep her both quiet and clean. Maybe someone who was a parent himself.

Pat made another note. Maybe they were looking for a couple, since taking things that belonged to the child sounded more like the actions of someone concerned for the child's welfare, someone like a mother.

He turned his attention to the pathologist's report. The probable cause of death was listed as blunt force trauma, inflicted when the back of the deceased's head had connected with the brickwork on the corner of the garden bed along the northern edge of the alfresco dining area at the rear of the house. Bruising on her upper arms and chest, fibres under her fingernails, and scuff marks on the tiles of the floor of the alfresco in the vicinity of the victim's body, suggested Sarah Taylor had been involved in some sort of tussle before she'd been pushed and fallen onto the edge of the garden bed.

Pat pushed his chair away from his desk. He needed a break before starting on the husband's statement, and going downstairs for a coffee would give him time to process what he'd just read.

CHAPTER 3

On Tuesday morning, Tessa King delivered her four-year-old daughter, Mia, to the Stirling Kindergarten, as she had each Tuesday since the start of the term. There was a huddle of mothers standing in the car park talking. Tessa walked Mia into the kindergarten and helped her hang her backpack on her assigned peg at the back of the classroom.

'Have a good day, sweetheart.'

'Bye, Mum.' Mia trotted over to join her classmates sitting cross-legged on the carpet square at the front of the room.

She's certainly settled in, thought Tessa, as she walked out to the car park where the same small group of mothers was still huddled. Tessa walked over to see what the meeting was about. What else could she do? She didn't want to draw attention to herself by ignoring them.

Fiona, one of the young mothers Tessa actually knew, turned as she joined the group. 'Tessa, have you heard about Sarah?'

'No. Has something happened?'

'It's been on all the morning news programs. She's dead.'

'What?'

'And, Ella's missing,' said one of the other mothers.

'The police spent half the night searching for her in the forest around their house,' said Fiona.

'Good God,' said Tessa. 'When did this happen?'

'Sam found her last night when he got home from the hospital.'

'Was there some sort of accident?' said Tessa.

'The police aren't saying. They're just saying she was dead when Sam got home and that Ella wasn't in the house.'

'Don't they have neighbours?'

'You can't see their nearest neighbour's house from their place. It's got to be a good two hundred metres away through the trees.'

'I wonder what happened to Sarah,' said Tessa. 'She wasn't ill, was she?'

'She was fine when I spoke to her at pick up time yesterday,' said Fiona.

'Yeah, she seemed okay to me, too,' said Tessa, shaking her head. 'It's going to be hot today, Ella's not going to last long if she's wandering around in the bush.'

The sound of the police helicopter sweeping overhead drowned out their conversation and they waited for it to recede into the distance.

'I think someone's taken her,' said Fiona, lowering her voice. 'Simon was up there with the SES last night until they called off the search.'

'I hope she's alright,' said Tessa. 'Perhaps we'll know more by pick up time.' Tessa turned to leave. 'I gotta go.'

Fiona smiled. 'Okay. See you later.'

Tessa walked over to her car and got in behind the wheel. Her hands were shaking. She wondered if bringing

Mia to the kindergarten this morning had been such a good idea after all, but Robbie and Jordan had insisted she stick to the plan.

She took a deep breath and hoped she'd be able to hold it together when she returned to pick up Mia later in the day. At least she wouldn't have to come back again until Friday. Hopefully, Ella would no longer be her problem by then.

On her way back to Balhannah, further east and more distant from the city, Tessa drove past the Stirling Aged Care Home. The place didn't look any different to when she'd worked there as a carer, up to the time the vaccine mandate had been introduced for aged care workers. She'd been stood down without pay when she'd refused to be vaccinated, despite the government calling out for aged care workers.

There was no way she was being a guinea pig for any Covid vaccines that had been developed in such an incredibly short time. She was okay with the regular vaccines that had been around for years, but there were too many people online with horror stories about what had happened to them after they had been vaccinated, including doctors saying that the Covid vaccines weren't safe. She just wasn't prepared to risk it. And, although she wasn't keen on wearing a face mask, she always wore one at the kindergarten to avoid a confrontation with the staff and other parents.

Robbie had lost his job as well, which meant they'd had to abandon the rental property in Peake Avenue, Stirling, where they'd lived for the last five years, and move in with her brother, Jordan, on the York family farm, located off Swamp Road, a few kilometres outside Balhannah.

It was Jordan who had alerted them to the dangers of the vaccines. At least there was no mandate insisting self-employed farmers be vaccinated, which meant Jordan still had an income. He'd also introduced them to the world of sovereign citizens, a world in which no-one had the right to tell anyone else what to do.

As she turned into the farm driveway fifteen minutes later, Tessa smiled to herself at the irony of the boys having to wear masks when they tended to Ella, who they'd secreted in the cellar under the apple storage shed, away from the house, so Mia wouldn't know she was there.

Tessa could not look after Ella. Even with a mask on, Ella would recognise her, since she'd befriended Mia, who had introduced her to Tessa at the end of the first day of kindergarten. Meeting Ella and her mother hadn't made any difference to Tessa, until Fiona had casually mentioned in passing that Sarah's father was the Police Commissioner, and she'd passed that information on to Robbie and Jordan.

They, of course, had immediately seen a way to get even with the Police Commissioner, who they held responsible for the imposition of the vaccine and mask mandates which had cost many of their friends and associates their jobs. Unfortunately, things hadn't quite gone to plan when they'd finally put all their talk into action. Sarah had put up a fight in an attempt to stop them abducting Ella. According to Robbie, she'd fallen and hit her head when he'd pushed her away so Jordan could grab Ella.

Neither of them knew anything useful about first aid, and calling an ambulance would have only complicated things, so they'd left her where she'd fallen, hoping she'd only knocked herself out.

They'd held a crisis meeting that morning when the

news of Sarah's death broke on the seven o'clock news. The boys were convinced they'd left nothing behind that could be used to identify them. They'd taken every precaution, worn gloves, pulled plastic bags over their boots, and covered their faces with surgical masks.

Over breakfast, they'd decided the best way forward would be for Tessa to take Mia to kindergarten as normal, while Jordan went to Mount Barker to post their letter of demand and stock up on ammunition for their hunting rifles. Robbie would stay at the farm and look after Ella.

Tessa knew Robbie wasn't happy about having to take care of their captive but, as Jordan had pointed out to him, he knew a lot more about looking after little girls than Jordan did.

CHAPTER 4

PAT RETURNED to his desk and read the husband's account of what he'd found when he'd arrived home from work and what he'd done immediately after.

It was obvious Sam Taylor had panicked and missed the signs indicating his daughter had been abducted, instead of wandering off into the surrounding woodland, until the crime scene investigators had walked him through the house. Pat shook his head. They'd wasted valuable time searching for Ella in the area around the house until Dr Taylor had realised the car seat was missing from his wife's car, along with some of his daughter's belongings.

Pat read the statements from the neighbours. Most of them hadn't been home between four and six that afternoon, and those that had been didn't recall seeing or hearing anything unusual or suspicious. It didn't help that the closest house was nearly two hundred metres away through dense woodland.

One residence in High Street had a security camera that captured a partial view of the street from its position on the front of the house. A review of the recording revealed two vehicles had gone past the end of the driveway in the direction of the Taylors' residence, within ten minutes of each other, just after four o'clock on the day of Sarah Taylor's murder.

The view was side on to the street, as the camera had been positioned to capture traffic coming up the driveway towards the house. The first car was a silver Mazda 3, based on its profile. Probably the same silver Mazda 3 parked in the Taylors' garage. The second vehicle appeared to be a white Toyota Hilux dual cab ute, a model popular with tradesmen, which was also captured going in the opposite direction twenty minutes later.

Pat reviewed the map of the area. High Street came to a dead end at the junction of driveways in front of the Taylors' house. Any vehicle which had proceeded beyond that point had either driven up the Taylors' driveway or that of their neighbour.

They didn't have many details on the vehicle but it looked like whoever had killed Sarah Taylor and abducted her daughter had driven away from the scene in a recent model white Toyota Hilux.

God, thought Pat, there must be thousands of white Toyota Hilux utes in the state.

His mobile pinged. It was a message from DI Ryan informing him the Commissioner had received a ransom demand and requesting his presence in the incident room on the fifth.

Derek Ryan was waiting for Pat when he entered the incident room. 'Good to see you, Pat. Been a while.'

Pat and Derek had worked together for several years under DCI Roberts when he'd been DI Roberts. They'd gone separate ways when Pat had taken leave following Pam's death and found himself detoured into cold case management when he'd returned to work.

'How are you, Derek? I hear they've made you an inspector.'

They shook hands, despite the Covid protocols insisting they shouldn't.

'They would have made you one if you'd stayed with us,' said Derek.

Pat laughed. 'Yeah, probably, but I'm happy where I am. I only have one officer reporting to me, not a whole bloody team like you have.'

'Tell me about it.'

'You got anyone looking for more camera footage from the surrounding streets?'

Derek nodded. 'Got a couple of young detectives scrolling through what we've got our hands on to date which, mind you, isn't much.' Derek shrugged. 'Got any idea how many bloody white Toyota utes there are on our roads, Pat? Thousands.'

'But they can't all have been in that part of Stirling on Monday afternoon.'

'True, but what we really need is some dashcam or traffic camera footage, and the only traffic cameras up there are on the freeway.'

'At least we know what we're looking for,' said Pat, feeling the familiar sense of camaraderie they'd enjoyed working together as sergeants. 'Now, what's in this ransom note?'

'Thought you'd never ask,' said Derek, giving Pat a dig in the ribs with his elbow.

Pat laughed and pushed him in the shoulder. 'They after money?'

'No. They're demanding an immediate end to both vaccine and mask mandates and a return to work for anyone stood down for not being vaccinated, and they want the government to provide them with backpay for the time they've been off work and, get this, they want the Commissioner sacked for imposing those mandates.'

Unusual list of demands, thought Pat. 'Is it signed?'

'By some group calling themselves Four Freedom using the numeral instead of the word.' Derek turned and wrote 4 Freedom on the white board behind them.

'Anti-vaxxers,' said Pat. 'Who's got the hard copy?'

'It's with Forensics.'

'Anything special about the letter itself?'

Derek pulled out his mobile, opened the message he'd received from DCI Roberts and showed Pat the photos of the letter and its envelope. 'All neatly typed up like any normal piece of correspondence.'

'Any idea where it was posted?'

'Still waiting to hear back from Australia Post.'

'Maybe that moniker will tell us something,' said Pat.

'Got someone looking at social media accounts,' said Derek. 'We might get lucky if they're an online group.'

'Did they set a deadline or say what would happen to the girl?'

'They want an answer by four pm Friday.'

'What about the girl?'

'Their threat's a bit vague. Words to the effect of if you value her life.'

'How are we meant to contact them?'

'They want a public announcement on ABC Radio Adelaide.'

'Sounds like they've given this some thought,' said Pat.

'Gonna be slow going if they're relying on Australia Post and us talking on ABC Radio,' said Derek, shaking his head.

'What do you need me to do?' said Pat.

'I thought you were supposed to be our intelligence review service.'

'Yeah, well there's not much to review yet,' said Pat, 'and I hear Covid's hit your team.'

'I could do with an extra pair of hands. How about you talk to the kindergarten to see if any of their parents are anti-vaxxers or knew Sarah Taylor was the Commissioner's daughter?'

CHAPTER 5

Pat arrived at Stirling Kindergarten at three-fifteen, as the stragglers from the Thursday afternoon session were leaving. He'd called the kindergarten's director, Rona Matthews, and she'd told him to come at the end of their day. As he entered the building, a tall woman, aged about fifty in Pat's estimation, with short greying hair intercepted him.

'Detective Sergeant Travers?'

'Yes,' said Pat, showing her his ID. 'I'm here to see Rona Matthews.'

'Come into my office.'

Pat took the seat offered, across from where Rona sat on the other side of the table that served as her desk, thinking she'd made sure he was appropriately distanced from her.

'Now, what was it you wanted to talk about, Sergeant?'

'Ella Taylor,' said Pat. 'I'm part of the team investigating her abduction and the death of her mother.'

'Absolutely shocking,' said Rona. 'Fortunately, our children are too young to fully understand what's happened, but it's been upsetting for the parents.'

'I'm sure it has,' said Pat. 'How long has Ella been attending?'

'This is her first term.'

'Is that the same for the other kids in her class?'

'She's in group A. They're all new this year.'

It was more than thirty years since Pat had had anything to do with kindergartens. 'Group A?'

'We divide our intake into two groups, Sergeant. Group A comes on Monday and Tuesday each week and every second Friday. Group B comes on Wednesday and Thursday and the alternate Friday to group A.'

'Ah, I vaguely remember kindergarten not being every day of the week,' said Pat. 'It's been a while since my kids were four-year-olds.'

'Same for me,' said Rona. 'Mine have kids of their own these days.'

'Mine haven't blessed me, yet,' said Pat. 'I'm still waiting to become a grandfather.'

Rona smiled.

'So, all of your parents would be new to the kindergarten as well?'

'Most of them, but some have had children here before.'

'How many kids in group A?'

'Fifteen this term.'

'Do any of your current group of parents express anti-vaxxer sentiments?' asked Pat.

'There's a government policy requiring children to be fully vaccinated to be enrolled,' said Rona. 'Came into effect in the middle of 2020.'

'There's no Covid vaccine for four-year-olds,' said Pat, 'so I guess it's possible someone who's become an anti-vaxxer because of Covid could still have immunised their kids against all the normal childhood diseases.'

'All I can tell you, Sergeant, is that our current cohort of children, including Ella, are fully immunised.'

'Haven't heard any whispers of anti-vaccine sentiment?'

Rona shook her head. 'No.'

'What about parents refusing to wear masks?'

'Where is this going, Sergeant?'

'We have reason to believe Ella is being held by an anti-vaccination group,' said Pat.

'Oh, I see.'

'So, any problems with mask wearers?'

'Not that I've noticed,' said Rona.

'I'm going to need to talk to the parents from group A,' said Pat.

'They'll be here tomorrow,' said Rona.

'Might be best if I speak to them individually,' said Pat. 'Can you give me a list of names and contact details?'

Pat waited while the director printed the details for him.

'Thanks,' said Pat, standing. 'Were you aware Sarah Taylor was the Police Commissioner's daughter?'

'I don't think that was a secret, Sergeant. Sarah had volunteered to get him to come and talk to the children about being a policeman.'

'So, everyone would have known?'

'Everyone at the parent meeting where we discussed who we could get to come and talk to the children about different jobs. I don't know about the others.'

Pat twisted his hands together. Finding the link was going to be a bit more of a challenge than he'd anticipated. 'Any chance I could have a word with Ella's teacher?'

'Not today, I'm afraid. She doesn't work Thursdays.'

'Perhaps I can catch her tomorrow,' said Pat.

'I could give you her mobile number, if you like, Sergeant?'

'That would be good.'

Pat parked outside the house at the address Mary Edwards had given him when she'd answered his call. It was a modest stone cottage with a roof of grey slate tiles marked with random patches of lichen. It looked old enough to have a heritage listing.

Pat leant on his car and admired the cottage. Its front wall was covered in ivy, the green leafed creeper climbing out of an untamed cottage garden of fading summer flowers. He pushed open a low wooden gate that looked as if it could do with a coat of paint and followed the path of crushed white stones to the relative coolness of the shade under the front verandah.

'Are you that policeman who called?'

Pat turned towards the sound of her voice and saw a middle-aged woman sitting at a round patio table in the corner of the verandah, where the shade was the deepest. 'I am.'

'Have a seat.'

Pat sat at the table and showed her his identification. 'Detective Sergeant Pat Travers. I take it you're Mary Edwards.'

The woman nodded. 'What do you want to know, Sergeant?'

'What can you tell me about Sarah Taylor, Ella's mother?'

'A little overprotective.' Mary smiled 'Took her a while to get used to leaving Ella with me but that's not unusual for first time mothers.'

'What was she like with the other parents?'

'Friendly enough,' said Mary. 'She was part of the parent support group.'

'What was she like on Monday, when she picked up Ella?'

'Ella didn't want to go home,' said Mary, smiling. 'It happens sometimes, especially with kids who don't have any siblings at home to play with, but Sarah was patient with Ella. We had a cuppa while Ella played.'

'She mention anything that might mean something now?'

Mary cocked an eyebrow. 'Like what?'

'Being followed home or feeling she was being watched.'

Mary shook her head. 'Nothing like that.'

'What time did she leave?'

'Around three forty-five, I think.'

'Anybody else about when she left?'

'The car park was empty apart from her car and mine.'

Pat scratched his head. 'When did you leave?'

'Around four-thirty, after I'd set things up for the following morning.'

'Dealing with the situation in the morning,' said Pat, imagining the shock she must have felt. 'That couldn't have been easy.'

'At least the children had no idea what was going on.'

Pat was glad he hadn't been the one trying to put on a happy face for the sake of the children. 'Ever hear any of the parents talking about the vaccine mandates or protesting about wearing masks?'

'Not at the kindergarten but I've seen a few people making a nuisance of themselves down at the shops.'

'Doing what?' said Pat.

'Refusing to sign in or wear masks and claiming no-one has the right to tell them what to do.'

'Anyone you recognise?'

Mary shook her head. 'Why are you interested in those sort of people?'

'Because it seems someone in that group is holding Ella,' said Pat.

'The poor little mite,' said Mary. 'Those people are crazy.'

'Oh, what makes you say that?'

'Ever tried talking to any of them, Sergeant?'

'Can't say that I have,' said Pat.

'I've got a sister who believes all that stuff. Thinks we've all got nano-chips in our arms and Bill Gates is taking over the world or some such rubbish. You can't reason with her. Anything you say contrary to her beliefs is fake news.'

'She live locally?' said Pat, thinking she might be a way into the local anti-vaxxer community.

'No, she lives in Sydney,' said Mary. 'Thank God. It's bad enough talking to her on the phone.' She looked at Pat. 'If you want to talk to any of the local nut cases, go down to the shops. You won't have any trouble working out who they are.'

CHAPTER 6

Friday morning started with a briefing in the incident room. Pat sat at the back of the room alongside DC Lina Palumbo, who was scanning the room.

'Who's the bald guy that looks like he could lose a few kilos?'

'That's DCI Roberts. He's the senior investigating officer.'

'Know anything about him, Pat?'

'I worked for him before I was transferred to Cold Cases.'

Before Lina could ask another question, a tall man, around Pat's age, dressed in a tailored dark grey suit, strode to the front of the room and called the team to order.

'That's DI Ryan,' said Pat. 'He's actually leading the investigation.'

Lina glanced at Pat and raised her eyebrows in that way which made him wish he was twenty years younger.

'Listen up, people,' said DI Ryan. 'The Commissioner will be on ABC Radio Adelaide this afternoon asking the kidnappers to make contact through Crime Stoppers. He won't be saying anything about the mandates they want lifted. That gives us until four o'clock to find these clowns.'

The officers in the room looked at each other in disbelief. Pat wondered if the kidnappers would be foolish enough to fall for the Commissioner's attempt to flush them out of their electronic hiding place.

'That ain't going to happen, sir,' said a young detective, sitting at a desk near the front of the room, 'unless we get extremely lucky. All we know about them is they drive what's got to be one of the most popular utes in the country.'

'We know they posted their ransom letter in a post box somewhere in Mount Barker,' said DI Ryan.

'They had to know the victim was the Commissioner's daughter and where she lived,' said a voice from the room.

'That suggests they're locals,' said DCI Roberts, 'or at least they have a local contact. Let's focus on people who lost their jobs because of the vaccine mandate and who's in any way connected to the victim.'

'Can you organise that search, Tim?' said DI Ryan, looking at DS Tim Healy.

'Right, sir. I'm on it.'

'Any luck finding 4 Freedom on social media?' said DI Ryan, looking at the young woman sitting at the computer in front of him.

'Plenty of references to four freedoms, sir, which is an American thing linked to a speech made by President Roosevelt in the nineteen forties. I haven't been able to find a local group using that name but there are plenty of anti-vaxxer groups online.'

'Okay, people. Keep looking.'

The briefing broke up with DS Healy assigning tasks to

expedite the search for anyone who had lost their job because they'd refused to be vaccinated.

'What are we doing?' said Lina, as they made their way down to the third floor.

'We're talking to the parents of the kids in Ella's kindergarten class, and then we'll see if we can meet some anti-vaxxers in downtown Stirling.'

Given their time constraints, Pat decided they'd call the parents of the fourteen other children in Ella's class and be present for the three o'clock pick up at the kindergarten to meet them in person. He and Lina divided the list and spent the morning placing and waiting for calls to be returned. By early afternoon, they'd spoken to at least one parent of each child and were on their way to the kindergarten in Stirling.

'Sounds like our victim was pretty friendly,' said Lina, 'and most people knew she was the Commissioner's daughter.'

'Only one of the women I spoke to, a Fiona Williams, said she knew where Sarah lived and had visited for a play date,' said Pat. 'Have any luck with that question?'

'Couple of mine,' Lina looked at her notes, 'Jenifer Rush and Hilary Wilde both said they'd been to her house.'

'That gives us at least three people who knew where she lived,' said Pat. 'Any luck with the anti-vaxxer question?'

'No, they all said they had to get their kids immunised to get them into the kindergarten, apparently that's the law these days.'

'No jab, no play,' said Pat.

'What about yours?'

'Same. Seems nobody talks about the mandates in this group.'

'Maybe we're wasting our time with these people,' said Lina. 'I can't really see anyone with young children kidnapping someone else's child.'

'Hard to imagine anti-vaxxers getting their kids immunised so they can send them to kindergarten,' said Pat.

'Unless they're recent converts to the cause,' said Lina. 'I hadn't heard of anti-vaxxers until Covid.'

'They've been around for a while,' said Pat. 'It's not only 5G and microchips they're worried about. There's a whole bunch of them claiming the measles vaccine causes autism and God only knows what else.'

'I feel like I've been living in a bubble,' said Lina.

'This stuff comes out of America,' said Pat, 'and it's been made worse by the QAnon conspiracy and all the bullshit around Trump.'

'Who ever thought their madness would take a hold here?' said Lina.

'At least we haven't taken on their crazy ideas about guns.'

'This 4 Freedom group might have,' said Lina. 'You watched any of that stuff about those people who stormed the Capitol building in Washington last year?'

'Can't help but see it if you watch TV,' said Pat, turning into the kindergarten car park. 'We're here.'

'What do you want to do?'

'Let's just stand outside the gate and wait and see if anyone wants to tells us anything else. They know we're going to be here.'

The parents of the Group A students arrived in an assortment of cars to collect their children from the kindergarten. Pat noticed none of them arrived in a white Toyota Hilux. Most of them simply acknowledged their presence on their way into the kindergarten to collect their child and ignored them on the way out.

Pat was surprised by the number of fathers collecting their offspring, until it occurred to him that maybe the mothers hadn't wanted another reminder of the tragedy by seeing the detectives who'd called them earlier in the day. As the car park was emptying, a young man holding the hand of a small girl with large brown eyes approached them.

'Detective Sergeant Travers?'

'Yes,' said Pat.

'Simon Williams. You spoke to my wife, Fiona, this morning.'

The girl ducked behind her father's legs and looked up at Pat with a shy smile. He winked at her and then looked at Simon. 'Has she remembered something?'

'She said you wanted to know if we'd heard any anti-vaccination talk around the kindergarten.'

'That's right.'

Simon glanced at Lina and smiled. 'I don't know if this will mean anything, but I heard on the grapevine that Robbie King, he's the father of one of the girls in Eva's class. Anyway, I heard he'd lost his job because he refused to get vaccinated.'

'Oh, what did he do for a job?'

'He drove a B-double hauling freight interstate.'

'Do you know who he worked for?'

'Imperial Freighters,' said Simon. 'I work for the firm that services their trucks.'

He might be our way into the anti-vaxxer community, thought Pat. 'Thanks, we'll follow that up.'

They waited in their car while Simon Williams loaded his daughter into the back seat of his car and drove out of the car park.

'The Kings were on your list. Who'd you talk to?'

'Tessa,' said Lina. 'She said she hadn't heard any talk about vaccine mandates.'

'Guess we asked her the wrong question,' said Pat. 'Where do they live?'

Lina consulted her copy of the list. 'In Peake Avenue.'

'Stick that address into the GPS and let's go and see if they're home.'

CHAPTER 7

TESSA ARRIVED home at five minutes to four, having stopped off at the supermarket in Balhannah to buy bread and milk. By the time she'd unloaded Mia and her shopping from the car, the introductory music announcing the four o'clock news on ABC Radio Adelaide was blaring out of the radio sitting on the mantle above the stove in the kitchen. 'You go in and watch TV,' said Tessa, guiding Mia down the passageway from the kitchen to the lounge room.

She joined Robbie and Jordan at the kitchen table, where they were nursing the dregs of their afternoon tea and waiting to hear the Commissioner's response to their demands.

After reading the weather details at the end of the news bulletin, the newsreader said, 'Please standby for a special announcement from the Police Commissioner.'

'This is a message for the people calling themselves 4 Freedom, who claim to have abducted Ella Taylor from her home in Stirling. I have received your letter and request that you make contact with my officers on 131444 to discuss your demands for Ella's return to her family.'

As ABC Radio Adelaide rolled into its afternoon line up, Tessa looked at her husband and brother. 'He didn't say anything about your demands.'

'They want to open lines of communication,' said Jordan, 'so they can track us down through our phones.'

'They're playing right into our hands,' said Robbie.

'What do you mean?' said Tessa, as her mobile phone started ringing. She picked up her phone and looked at the number calling. 'It's that detective that called earlier.'

'Let it go through to voicemail,' said Jordan, 'and don't call her back until I tell you.'

Tessa put her phone on the table.

'Do you think they're on to us already?' said Robbie.

'Can't see how,' said Jordan, 'but even if they are, it won't make any difference.'

'What?' said Tessa, feeling confused.

'They're never going to agree to our demands,' said Jordan. 'They'll sacrifice the kid because they think their mandates are keeping people alive, people who vote in their precious elections.'

'What are we going to do with Ella?' said Tessa. 'We can't keep her forever.'

Robbie and Jordan exchanged a meaningful glance. Tessa felt a constriction in her chest.

'We're going to use her as bait,' said Jordan, 'and then kill us a shit load of cops when they finally work out where she is.'

'Oh,' said Tessa. 'And, then what?'

'All this madness will be over,' said Jordan. 'We'll be dead.'

'What if I don't want that?' said Tessa, realising they

35

hadn't even bothered to find out if she agreed with their plan or not.

'Why wouldn't you?' said Robbie. 'There's nothing for us here with all these arseholes telling us what to do. I've had enough, and I don't want Mia living in a world like that.'

Tessa looked at her hands on the table in front of her and then dropped them into her lap to stop them from shaking. 'So, what's the plan?'

'We play for time,' said Jordan. 'We keep them guessing until we're ready.'

'And, when will that be?' said Tessa.

'When I say,' said Jordan.

'I assume Mia won't be going to kindergarten next week,' said Tessa.

'Both of you will be staying here,' said Robbie, 'unless I tell you otherwise.'

'So is there any point keeping Ella locked in the storage shed?' said Tessa. 'It'd be easier to look after her if she was in the house with Mia.'

'Go and get her if it makes you feel better,' said Jordan, 'but make sure she stays where you can keep an eye on her.'

'And, don't go getting any bright ideas,' said Robbie, pocketing her phone.

Tessa walked up the incline to the apple storage shed. It was a stone building with a high galvanised iron roof that her great-grandfather had built when he'd established the orchard. She stood in front of the shed and took in the view of apple trees spread across the hillside as far as she could see. It was a sight that always filled her with pride. Her family had worked hard to establish the orchard and make a living for themselves on this patch of earth for nearly a hundred years. She wasn't ready to walk away from it, no matter what Jordan and Robbie said. There had to be something she could do to save herself and the girls before it was too late.

Robbie had been friends with Jordan since high school. That's how she'd met him. The boys had always been as thick as thieves, and they'd only become closer since she and Robbie had moved back to the farm after losing their jobs. As she opened the heavy wooden door of the shed, she wondered if she would have made the same decision about the vaccine if she'd been on her own, away from the influence of Robbie and her brother.

She'd always done what Robbie had told her to do, believed what he said was true. She was too frightened of him not to. He had a temper she'd learnt not to trigger. As she lifted the trapdoor to the cellar, she wondered if Sarah's death had really been an accident or if Robbie had taken pleasure in beating her to death as she'd tried to protect her child.

Ella looked up from her toys as Tessa descended the stairs. It was cool in the cellar, which was illuminated by the diffused light allowed in from a small window on the southern wall away from the sun. The place smelt like a toilet in need of a flush to Tessa, and she realised neither of the boys had been in to check on Ella since lunch time.

'Hello, sweetheart,' said Tessa, wrapping her arms around Ella.

'Where's Mummy?' said Ella.

'She's busy,' said Tessa. 'I've come to look after you. Do you want to play with Mia?'

Ella nodded at the sound of her friend's name.

'Just let me gather your things,' said Tessa, picking up her toys and dropping them into the sports bag holding her clothes. 'Come on. I think you could do with a bath. Would you like that?'

'Can I have a bath with Mia?'

'I can't see why not.'

CHAPTER 8

'You have arrived at your destination, on the left.' The posh English voice of the navigation system made Pat smile. It was so out of place, especially on a day hot enough for even a mad dog to be looking for shade. He parked the car in the shade of the street tree in front of the house.

There was a white Toyota Hilux parked in the driveway, behind a bright blue Hyundai i30 sitting under the carport.

'Looks like someone is home,' said Lina.

Pat snapped a shot of the number plate on the Toyota, before joining Lina on the verandah, where she was pressing the button for the doorbell.

The door was opened by a woman old enough to be Lina's mother. 'How can I help you, love?'

Lina showed the woman her identification. 'We're looking for Robbie and Tessa King.'

The woman smiled. 'They were the previous tenants. We've been here since early October.'

'Do you have a forwarding address for them?' said Lina.

'No, but the property manager must,' said the woman. 'She asked us to drop off any mail for the Kings at her office.'

'Who's your property manager?'

'Her name's Karen Fisher. Her office is in the shopping centre behind the Stirling Hotel. You can't miss it. It's got a big photo of her on the front window.'

'Who drives the Toyota?' said Pat.

'My husband,' said the woman. 'Why?'

'Can we have a word with him?'

The woman shrugged. 'I suppose.' She poked her head inside the door and called to her husband to come out and talk to the police. After a short delay, a man with long grey hair pulled back into a ponytail appeared in the doorway.

'This your vehicle?' said Pat, pointing to the Toyota.

'Yeah.'

'Mind telling me where your vehicle was between four and six last Monday afternoon?'

'Why do you want to know that?'

'We're investigating the abduction of Ella Taylor,' said Pat, 'and a vehicle similar to yours was seen leaving the scene around the time we think she was taken.'

'I see,' said the man. 'Process of elimination, is it? You've certainly got a lot of these utes to check out, haven't you? Glad it's you not me. Anyway, I had a doctor's appointment at four. I didn't get out of there until close to five and, by the time I'd waited at the chemist, it would have been around twenty to six when I got home.'

Pat looked at the woman.

'I was at work. I'm a domestic at the hospital. I was on the late afternoon shift until yesterday.'

'Perhaps you can show me your licence and tell me which doctor you saw,' said Pat.

'Sure,' said the man, pulling his wallet out of the back pocket of his jeans.

The young woman sitting at the desk in the office of Karen Fisher Property Management looked up when Pat opened the door. 'Can I help you?'

'I hope so,' said Pat, showing her his identification. 'I'm Detective Sergeant Travers.'

'I guess you're not looking for a rental property, then.'

'No,' said Pat, 'and your name would be?'

'Oh, sorry, I'm Natalie Fisher. What is it you're after?'

'Do you have a forwarding address for Tessa and Robbie King?'

'Are they previous tenants?' said Natalie. 'Which property?'

'5 Peake Avenue.'

'Give me a minute.' Natalie turned to the computer on her desk and tapped on her keyboard. 'We've only got a post office box in Balhannah, I'm afraid. PO Box 36.'

'That will give me somewhere to start,' said Pat, writing the details in his notebook. 'Do you have a record of where Tessa King worked?'

Natalie tapped a few more keys. 'She was working at the Stirling Aged Care Home, that's on Old Mt Barker Road, according to this.'

Pat wrote that detail in his notebook. 'Did they give a reason for leaving?'

Natalie shook her head. 'Decided not to renew their lease when it came up for renewal last year.'

Pat closed his notebook. 'Thanks, you've been a great help.'

Pat walked back to the car and got in. 'We need to go to the Stirling Aged Care Home on Old Mt Barker Road.'

Lina keyed the address into the navigation system.

The Stirling Aged Care Home, a large house with several outbuildings, all constructed of local stone and surrounded by an extensive garden with numerous mature trees, had the hallmarks of being a repurposed grand building from colonial times. Pat walked through the gardens and didn't realise he hadn't thought his visit through until he reached the front door. It was locked, and there was a notice in the glass pane of the door informing him that, under the home's Covid protocols, only staff members were permitted to enter the building, provided they had tested negative to Covid in the prior 72 hours.

Pat called the number displayed at the bottom of the notice.

'How can I help you?' said a woman's voice.

'I'm Detective Sergeant Pat Travers,' said Pat. 'I'm looking for Tessa King.'

'Can you hold up your identification, Sergeant? There's a camera just above you.'

Pat looked up, and then held his identification up to the camera.

'Thank you, Sergeant, but I'm afraid you've wasted your time. Tessa's been on indefinite leave since September last year. She refused to be vaccinated and we had to stand her down.'

Pat wondered how vocal Tessa had been. 'Did she try to talk any of the others into not being vaccinated?'

'Not to my knowledge. She just told us she wasn't

prepared to risk it, which was a shame. She was a good worker. The residents loved her.'

'Thanks.' Pat slipped his phone into his pocket and walked back to the car.

'Any luck?' said Lina.

'She lost her job for not being vaccinated,' said Pat. 'Has she called you back?'

'Not yet.'

Pat looked at his watch. 'Guess we'd better head back. You drive, I need to talk to Derek.'

CHAPTER 9

PAT ARRIVED at the Saturday morning briefing with only a minute to spare. He'd had to skip his morning coffee to make it, after catching a later bus than he'd planned when the seven-fifteen bus hadn't arrived at all. Driver shortage due to Covid was the excuse the driver of the seven-thirty bus had given him. And, it looked like Covid had hit a few more members of the team, going by the number of officers in the incident room.

'DS Travers has had some luck speaking to the parents of the children at Ella's kindergarten,' said DI Ryan. 'We may have a possible link between the anti-vaxxers and our victim. The parents of Mia King, Robbie and Tessa King. Apparently both have been stood down from their employment for refusing to be vaccinated.'

'Have we spoken to these people?' said DCI Roberts.

'We've had one phone conversation with Tessa,' said Pat, 'prior to learning about their employment situation. She told us she hadn't heard any anti-vaxxer talk among the parents, and none of the other parents we spoke to mentioned anything about her being an anti-vaxxer herself.'

'One of the quiet ones,' said DI Ryan.

'They've had their daughter vaccinated against the normal range of childhood diseases,' said Pat. 'It's a condition of enrolment at kindergartens.'

'Recent converts to the cause, then,' said DI Ryan. 'Anyway, I've had some background checks run on them. No record of convictions, and neither of them is registered as the owner of a Toyota Hilux, but Robbie is the registered owner of a single shot hunting rifle. One thing that's interesting is they haven't updated their address with Registrations.'

'That could just be an oversight,' said a voice from the room.

'Bit outside the fourteen day window, though. They left their last known address last September,' said Pat. 'How'd you go with the post office box, sir?'

'Still chasing that up,' said DI Ryan. 'Mt Barker is sending someone over this morning. It's one of those licensed post offices. They open this morning at nine.' He looked at his watch. 'Should have something in the next fifteen minutes or so.'

'She called us back yesterday morning but she hasn't returned our calls since,' said Pat. 'Perhaps we should try and locate her using her phone.'

'Do you have a number for the father?' said DI Ryan.

'Not yet,' said Pat. 'I'll follow up with his employer when we finish here. The kindergarten only had a number for the mother.'

'Okay, let Tim know when you have it and, Tim, get someone onto the phone logs and position data.'

'Right, sir,' said DS Healy.

'The rest of you, keep looking for that Toyota. Someone has to have seen it.'

As soon as they got back to their office on the third, Pat called Imperial Freighters.

'I'm not sure I can divulge that information, mate.'

'Would you like me to come down with a warrant and search through your files?' said Pat.

Silence. Pat waited. He heard the sound of keys being tapped.

'0417 825 398.'

Pat wrote down the number and handed it to Lina. 'Have you heard from him since he was stood down?'

'Nah, but I hope he comes to his senses soon. We need drivers.'

'So, you'd have him back when the mandate is lifted?'

'We'd have him back now if he'd get the bloody jab. He was one of our more reliable drivers. Been with us for five years.'

'Okay, thanks for your help.' Pat wondered what else was going on at Imperial Freighters they didn't want him to know about, but let it slide. Finding Ella was their priority for now. He called the number he'd been given for Robbie King.

'The number you have called is either out of range or has been switched off. Please leave a short message after the beep.'

Pat left his details and asked Robbie to call him back. As soon as he'd put his phone down it started ringing.

'Pat, that post office box is registered to a Jordan York. His address is York Orchard, Swamp Road, Balhannah, and he's the registered owner of a white Toyota Hilux. Mt Barker has sent a patrol to get a statement from him.'

'Do you think that's wise, Derek?'

'There's nothing about him on the system, Pat.'

'Does he own any firearms?'

'A single shot hunting rifle. I've passed that information onto Mt Barker.'

'I guess we'll just have to wait and see what he has to say.'

CHAPTER 10

ALERTED BY THE sound of the alarm, triggered by a vehicle passing through the entrance of the driveway leading up to the farm buildings, Jordan York looked up from his morning tea to check the screen of the security system monitor. The image on the display showed a police patrol car approaching the house.

'Robbie! Get Tessa and the kids into the cellar, and tell her to keep them quiet!'

Jordan waited for Tessa and the girls to disappear down the steps into the cellar. 'Lock the door, mate. We don't want any surprises.'

'What's up?' said Robbie.

'Couple of cops coming up the driveway. Come on, let's find out what they want. Let me do the talking.'

By the time they'd walked out into the yard, the patrol car had come to a stop behind Jordan's Toyota and two young constables were getting out of it.

'How can I help you?' said Jordan, standing with his hands in his pockets.

'Which one of you is Jordan York?' said the taller of the constables.

'I'm Jordan.'

'Who's your friend?'

'This is my brother-in-law, Robbie King. Why are you here?'

'We've been asked to confirm whether Robbie and his wife are living here,' said the constable.

'Well, you can see that they are. Is that all you want?'

'Can you tell me where this vehicle was on Monday afternoon, Mr York, say from four o'clock onwards?'

'It was here. It's my work vehicle. Robbie and I didn't leave the property on Monday.'

'Is that right, Mr King?'

'Yep,' said Robbie.

'What about Mrs King? Did she leave the property on Monday afternoon?'

Jordan turned to Robbie and waited.

'She went to get our daughter from the kindergarten in Stirling, but she was back before four.'

'She drive the Toyota?'

'Nah, that's her car over there.' Robbie pointed to the silver Honda Civic parked next to an ancient Massey Ferguson tractor in the equipment shed on the other side of the yard.

'Okay, thanks,' said the constable. 'I understand there are some detectives wanting to speak with you and your wife, Mr King. Might pay to turn your phone on if you don't want them coming out to knock on your door.'

'Right,' said Robbie. 'I'll do that.'

'Oh, and Mr King, you might want to attend to updating your address with Service SA within the next fourteen days.'

'Will do,' said Robbie.

The constables got into their patrol car and made their way back up the driveway to the road.

'What do you reckon?' said Robbie.

'They've got no idea.'

'They seem to know about the ute,' said Robbie. 'Some-body must have seen us.'

'They obviously didn't get anything identifying us,' said Jordan, 'otherwise they'd have been here before today, and they certainly wouldn't have sent a couple of plods from Mt Barker.'

'Do you think we should return their calls?'

'Probably be a good idea if we don't want then poking about until we're ready for them, but you do it. I don't want Tessa saying anything she shouldn't.'

'She'll do what I tell her, mate. She always does.'

'Why are we in the cellar, Mummy?

'We're hiding,' said Tessa.

'Why?'

'Daddy wants us to hide.'

'Why?'

'So he can find us.'

'Why is Ella hiding with us?'

'Because she's staying with us.'

'Why?'

'Because her mummy is busy.'

'Where's her daddy.'

'At the 'ospedal,' said Ella. 'He's always busy.'

'That's right,' said Tessa.

'What's Daddy doing now?' said Mia.

'He's looking for us.'

The door to the cellar opened.

'Quick, hide!' said Tessa, and laughed as the girls ran and hid behind the boxes in the far corner.

'What's so funny?' said Robbie, as he came down the stairs.

'They're hiding from you,' said Tessa, pointing to the boxes. 'Go on, go over and find them.'

Robbie crept over to the boxes and looked over the top of the pile. 'Boo!'

The girls ran to Tessa and she gathered them in her arms. 'Come on. Let's go upstairs and have something to eat.'

Tessa set the girls up in front of the TV with a plate of snacks and turned on the kids channel. Then she went back into the kitchen where her husband was reading the paper.

'What was that about?'

'What?' said Robbie, putting down the paper.

'Forcing us into the cellar and locking the door.'

'Couple of coppers out in the yard. Didn't want young Ella making a dash for it.'

Yeah, right, thought Tessa. 'What did they want?'

'They wanted to see if you and I were living here,' said Robbie.

'Perhaps we should have returned that call yesterday.'

Robbie took out his phone. 'I've got a message from some Detective Sergeant. I'll give him a call and see what they want.'

'They wanted to know if we knew any anti-vaxxers,' said

Tessa. 'I said we didn't. Perhaps they've found out why we lost our jobs.'

'That might explain how they got my number,' said Robbie.

'What are you going to tell them?'

Robbie picked up the paper and smiled. 'Nothing.'

CHAPTER 11

PAT WAS HAVING a morning coffee with Lina in the coffee shop across the road from the police building when Derek Ryan joined them.

'How's the old warhorse treating you, Lina?'

'Who's calling who old here?' said Pat.

'He's taking good care of me,' said Lina. 'I gather you two have worked together before.'

'We go way back,' said Derek. 'If you ever want any background on Pat, come and see me. I'll set you straight.'

'Don't listen to him, Lina. He's full of shit.'

'And you aren't?'

'Can I get you a coffee, sir?' said Lina.

'You've got this one well trained, Pat,' said Derek, giving Pat a dig in the ribs. 'I'll have a flat white to go, no sugar, thanks.'

Pat and Derek watched Lina make her way over to the counter to order Derek's coffee.

'She good value, Pat? I've heard a few disparaging whispers among the troops.'

'You can ignore that bullshit, mate. She's ruffled a few of the old boys and they don't like it.'

'She'll go far then,' said Derek, 'especially with you coaching her. Now, down to business. I've just heard from Mt Barker. They've confirmed the Kings are living at the Balhannah property and they sighted York's Toyota. According to York, he and King didn't leave the property on Monday.'

'At least we know where to look for them if they don't return our calls.'

'The attending officers reported seeing at least four cameras along the driveway as they drove into the property and three others covering the yard between the house and the outbuildings.'

'Interesting,' said Pat. 'Didn't know apples were that valuable.'

'Maybe he's had some fuel thefts or people pinching his equipment,' said Derek. 'Remember that case we had outside Gawler?'

'You two reminiscing?' said Lina, placing Derek's coffee on the table.

'Trying to work out why York has so many security cameras,' said Pat.

'Maybe he's just paranoid,' said Lina.

'That, or he's got something more valuable than apples stored on his farm,' said Derek, picking up his coffee. 'Let me know what you find out from the Kings.'

———

They'd just left the coffee shop when Pat's mobile rang.

'Detective Sergeant Travers.'

'Robbie King returning your call, Sergeant.'

'Thanks for calling back, Robbie. You okay to answer a couple of questions?'

'That might depend on what they are,' said Robbie. 'What is it you want to know?'

'We've been told you were stood down by your employer because of the vaccine mandate. Is that right?'

'Yeah, but what's that got to do with anything?'

That sounded a little defensive to Pat, who wanted to keep Robbie talking, not get his back up. 'You're aware Ella Taylor's been kidnapped, aren't you?'

'Yeah, my daughter goes to the same kindergarten.'

'It's not public knowledge yet, Robbie, but she's being held by people who share your views on the Covid vaccine.'

'How do you know that?'

'They sent us a letter. Have you or your wife heard of an anti-vaccine group called 4 Freedom?'

'Just a minute.'

Pat heard Robbie asking Tessa if she'd heard of the group and her denying it.

'No. We don't belong to any anti-vaxxer groups, Sergeant. We did our own research. Made up our own minds.'

Pat wondered how true that statement was, given the plethora of anti-vaxxer groups spewing misinformation across social media that he knew about, but decided to give Robbie the benefit of the doubt and not to press him on the matter.

'Do you know anybody else that belongs to an anti-vaxxer group who might be prepared to talk to me?'

'Nah, we keep to ourselves.'

'Are you worried about your ongoing employment prospects?' said Pat, trying to gauge Robbie's views on the vaccine mandate.

'It's a bit rough making ends meet at the moment, mate, which is why we're living with my wife's brother, but these mandates won't last forever. I'll get my job back. The boss keeps ringing me, begging me to change my mind.'

That's basically what Robbie's boss had told him, thought Pat. 'Well, thanks for returning my call and good luck with getting your job back.'

Pat ended the call.

'What did he say?' said Lina.

'Claims they don't know of or belong to any anti-vaxxer groups, and he sounds philosophical about getting his job back once the mandates expire.'

'So, not someone angry enough to kidnap the Commissioner's grand-daughter to demand his job back?'

'Didn't sound like it.'

'So, we're no closer to solving this?'

'We need to hope someone got a shot of the number plate of that Toyota in the vicinity of the Taylors' house.'

'I was sure the Kings would be the link,' said Lina. 'Guess there must be some other anti-vaxxers connected to that kindergarten.'

'Or the hospital where Dr Taylor works.'

'You saying it could be a family member of someone who died from Covid with a vendetta against the doctor,' said Lina, 'and all this stuff about mandates and job losses is just a distraction?'

Pat shrugged. 'Anything's possible, Lina.'

'What do we do now?'

'Guess I'd better bring Derek up to date.'

Pat called DI Ryan and briefed him on what Robbie King had told him. 'He was pretty philosophical about the vaccine mandate and getting his job back, Derek. Didn't sound like someone who'd go out of his way to demand an end to the mandate.'

'Tim's got people following up with the families of any unvaccinated patients that died out at Flinders, Pat, but Dr Taylor denies being threatened by anyone about the death of a Covid patient,' said DI Ryan. 'I'll get the statements sent through for you to review, but while you're waiting for that, perhaps you and Lina can join the group going through the video footage that's been coming in. Get Tim to explain the video log before you start.'

Pat and Lina went up to the fifth floor and found DS Healy, who explained the system he'd set up for tracking video files and recording findings.

'You should be able to access the files from your desk downstairs,' said DS Healy. 'That way you'll be able to focus away from all the distractions up here.'

'How many files are there, Tim?' said Pat.

'How long's a piece of string?' said DS Healy. 'We're getting new recordings every day.'

As they were making their way downstairs, Pat's mobile rang. He glanced at the caller ID. The call was from his mother. Something had to be wrong for her to be calling him at work

'You go ahead, Lina. I'll catch up with you in a moment. It's my mother.'

Lina shook her head and smiled. Pat had told her about his mother on one of their long drives to Burra, during the first case they'd worked on together earlier in the year.

CHAPTER 12

PAT'S PARENTS were in their eighties. They'd been in their thirties when he was born and hadn't gifted him any siblings. Being an only child had had its upside when he was younger, but now it meant he was on his own whenever life presented his parents with a challenge.

'Hello, Mum.'

'Your father's driven the car into the back of the garage.'

This could be serious, thought Pat, after he'd gotten over the shock of the directness of her statement, without any words of greeting or warning. 'Is he hurt?'

'I don't know. He won't answer me.'

God, I hope he hasn't killed himself, thought Pat. That would really set the cat among the pigeons; there was no way his mother could take care of herself without assistance. 'Where are you, Mum?'

'We're trapped in the bloody car waiting for the ambulance to arrive.'

Thank God she's had the sense to call an ambulance, thought Pat. 'Are you alright, Mum?'

'I'm not hurt, I just can't get out of the bloody car.'

That could mean anything, thought Pat. His mother was into denial about her health at the best of times. She was never sick, even when her doctor had her on antibiotics or in a hospital bed. 'What about Dad?'

'I think he must have hit his head.'

Pat didn't want to think what that might look like. 'Is he breathing?'

'I think so, but the silly bugger's somewhere under the bloody airbag. I can't see his face.'

'When did you call the ambulance?' said Pat, wondering if she'd also been knocked unconscious on impact.

'Just before I called you. Can you come and help me get out of this bloody car?'

She sounded alert. 'Hang tight, Mum. I'm on my way.'

Pat called a taxi, ducked into the squad room to tell Lina where he'd be, and then went down to wait for the taxi in front of the building, wishing he'd driven his car into the office that morning instead of catching the bus.

When Pat arrived at his parents' place in Norwood, there was a fire truck and two vehicles in the livery of the Ambulance Service parked in the street. A small crowd of concerned elderly neighbours stood on the footpath in front of the house. The crew from the fire service was operating a device that looked like an oversized can opener on the driver's side of his father's car, which they'd pulled out of the partially demolished garage into the driveway. A team of paramedics was attending to the occupants of the vehicle through the rear door of the passenger's side.

Pat peered into the wreckage of the garage. There was a

gash in the trunk of the oak tree his father had planted behind the garage when they'd purchased the house fifty-five years ago, two years before he'd been born. The car had obviously hit the back wall of the garage at speed and come to an abrupt halt against the tree.

Pat shook his head. His mother would still have been wearing her seat belt. She was a stickler for the rules and had always insisted on not releasing her seat belt until the car had come to a final stop inside the garage. His father, on the other hand, had gotten into the habit of releasing his seat belt as soon as he'd turned into their street. What she called his reckless disregard for life had driven his mother mad. They'd had untold arguments about leaving your seat belt fastened until the car had come to a stop. Pat's father had not been persuaded. He'd probably never hear the end of it now, if he survived, thought Pat.

He introduced himself to one of the paramedics standing next to the ambulance and asked about the condition of his parents.

'Your mother's probably got a broken collarbone and bruised ribs, and damage to her lower limbs. We won't know for sure until we get her out, but her legs are trapped where the engine's been pushed back into the car. We've given her something to block the pain, so you won't be able to talk to her, I'm afraid.'

God, and she still managed to make those phone calls and claim she was okay, thought Pat. 'What about my dad?'

'Hard to say. He wasn't wearing a seat belt when they hit the wall and he's been knocked unconscious. Looks like the airbag hit him in the face, but he could have broken legs and internal injuries as well. At least he's breathing.'

Pat wondered if they'd survive, and what that might

mean for him if they couldn't look after themselves when they did.

'Clear!'

Pat snapped back into the present at the call and turned his attention to the action around the car, where the fire service crew were disengaging their device and stepping back to allow the paramedics to extract their patients from the twisted wreckage, which had once been Pat's father's pride and joy. He watched as his parents were loaded onto gurneys and then into the back of the waiting ambulances.

'Which hospital?' said Pat.

'The Royal Adelaide,' said the paramedic, 'and let's hope we don't have to spend too much time on the ramp.'

'Good luck with that,' said Pat. Ramping was now a fact of life, thanks to the increased demand for hospital beds driven by the pandemic and a range of other little understood issues within the health system. Pat was glad he was investigating crime and not trying to solve the problems of the health system but, at the same time, he didn't want the system to fail his parents in their hour of need.

CHAPTER 13

TESSA LISTENED as Robbie spoke to the detective on the phone and wondered what their plan really was. He certainly didn't sound like someone using Ella as bait to lure the police into an ambush or whatever it was he and Jordan had in mind.

'What's going on, Robbie? I thought you wanted them to know we had Ella.'

Robbie shrugged. 'They didn't even ask. Besides, we're not ready for them yet.'

'What do you mean, not ready?'

'Jack's promised me a semi-automatic and other stuff. We're not doing this on our own. This is going to be a statement for the movement.'

Fuck your bloody movement, thought Tessa. 'Did you ever think to ask me whether I wanted to be a part of this statement?'

Robbie stared at her, with that look on his face that told her she'd stepped over the line. Tessa held her breath and waited, feeling herself retreating into that place deep within her soul where she'd run to so many times before.

'I'm the head of this household, Tessa. I decide what's best for us. I don't have to ask you.'

'But you could have?' said Tessa, doing her best not to succumb to the urge to run from the room.

'You know the teaching, Tessa. Wives submit to your husbands.' He curled his fingers to form air quotes about the words. 'It wasn't a problem when you agreed to it as part of our marriage vows, why should it be a problem now?' He glared at her and twisted his right fist into the palm of his left hand. 'Now fix me something to eat. I have to go to the city after lunch to sort things out with Jack.'

'Jordan going with you?' said Tessa, turning towards the kitchen so her face wouldn't betray her feelings. 'Will he be wanting lunch now, too?'

'Nah, he's staying here in case the police come snooping.'

And to keep an eye on me, thought Tessa.

Tessa thought about her predicament as she set about making sandwiches for Robbie's lunch. She'd never possessed any real courage. A shy child, she'd been bullied at school, where she'd learnt the art of being the invisible one, especially around boys like her brother, Jordan, and his mates. Jordan, who was five years older than Tessa, had treated her as more of a nuisance than a little sister, until he'd found a use for her in her teenage years.

He'd plied her with alcohol and passed her around among his mates, telling her to keep her legs open and her mouth shut. Although he'd threatened often, he'd only ever hit her once. That was on the night of their parents' funeral, when she'd been eighteen and foolish enough to tell him she wanted to leave home. She'd been his housekeeper after that, right up until the day four years later when she'd married Robbie, and they'd moved into the house in Stirling.

Living with Robbie had turned out to be more enjoyable than living with Jordan, even though he treated her more as a sex slave than a wife whenever he was home. But, he was away a lot with work and he had encouraged her to get a job to help fill in the time when he wasn't home. With no post-school qualifications, she'd ended up working as a cleaner at the old folks home where, after some part-time study, she'd become a carer.

She'd fallen pregnant during one of Robbie's sex filled weekends at home, the same year she'd transitioned into the carer role. Initially, Robbie had been angry about the pregnancy. He hadn't been keen on the idea of having kids but, surprisingly, her life had taken a turn for the better following the birth of their daughter, Mia. Robbie was immediately besotted with her, which meant Tessa got more time to herself whenever he was home and Mia was awake.

The birth of Mia had given Tessa a new focus in life, another being to love who loved her back unconditionally. Tessa hadn't experienced that level of love from anyone, certainly not from her mother, who'd made sure Tessa understood she'd been a mistake from the moment she'd been born, right up to the day her parents had died in a car crash on the freeway.

She'd also seen another side of Robbie, a softer and more considerate persona, one he'd never really shared with her before Mia had come along. However, it hadn't stopped him controlling everything about her life. He was obsessed with being the head of the household in the fundamentalist Christian sense, even though they no longer attended Church on a regular basis.

Although she and Robbie had both had jobs, they'd never accumulated any significant savings, thanks to their lifestyle spending choices. Consequently, when their decision to refuse the Covid vaccine had cost them their jobs, they'd been forced to seek refuge in the York family home with Jordan, who'd never married. He'd been happy about them moving in and Tessa resuming her duties as housekeeper, while Robbie helped out in the orchard and played with Mia.

It had been Jordan who'd encouraged them to do their own research on the vaccines and who'd sent them links to websites and videos pushing claims of the vaccine being too experimental and dangerous for them to take. They'd spent countless hours discussing everything they could find on the vaccine, and decided it just wasn't safe, even though they'd never questioned the safety of any other vaccines before Covid came along.

Despite what they'd read about Covid being a hoax, Tessa had convinced Robbie and Jordan that it was real. She'd witnessed what Covid had done to some of the elderly residents of the nursing home where she'd worked. She just couldn't bring herself to take the vaccine in light of the pressure she'd come under from Robbie and Jordan. They'd been very persuasive but, in those moments when she was alone with herself, she knew she'd gone along with the anti-vaccine message out of fear of her husband and her brother, who were convinced it was all a conspiracy by the authorities intent on controlling everyone.

It wasn't just the pandemic measures that had Robbie and Jordan fired up. They'd joined 4 Freedom, a sovereign citizens group, and dragged Tessa and Mia along to a series of protests demanding the restoration of their freedoms and the end of mandates. Tessa hadn't been convinced, but she'd experienced the consequences of resisting often enough to know it wasn't safe to refuse when Robbie said she had to do something, so she'd dutifully gone along to the protests.

She was thankful they hadn't been arrested. The protests had been illegal gatherings, since the sovereign citizens leading them didn't believe in getting authorisation to hold a protest. She was sure they'd been photographed and was amazed the police hadn't brought that up during their interviews.

Tessa came out of her reverie as she slid the plate of sandwiches she'd prepared for Robbie onto the table in front of him. 'Do you think the police will suspect us if they see us in the photos they took at those protests we went to?'

Robbie looked up from the sandwich he'd reached for and shook his head. 'Needle in a haystack, Tessa. They're looking for a non-existent group of anti-vaxxers and trying to work out who was driving a Toyota like Jordan's. They haven't got time to be looking at photos of people protesting about threats to their personal freedom.'

'Where are the girls?' said Tessa, not wanting to argue with him, since he was always right.

'Jordan took them to feed the ducks on the dam.'

'Well, I guess they'll be back soon looking for something to eat themselves,' said Tessa, turning her attention to the task of preparing their lunch.

When Robbie departed for his meeting in the city, Tessa ran across to the implement shed and secured Ella's car seat next to Mia's on the back seat of her car. Then, she returned to the house and opened the control panel of the security system and muted the alarm connected to the sensor at the entrance of the driveway.

She was back in the kitchen, making sandwiches, when the girls burst in brimming over with excitement.

'Mum! We saw a snake!' said Mia, her brown eyes wide.

'A big black one!' said Ella, stretching her hands out as wide as she could.

'Uncle Jordan picked us up so it couldn't get us!' said Mia.

'It went in the grass!' said Ella.

'You were lucky you were with Uncle Jordan,' said Tessa. 'Now you know why you can't go up to the dam on your own.'

'Will it come back?' said Mia.

'I hope not,' said Tessa. 'Now go and wash your hands for lunch.'

Tessa stood in the doorway of the bathroom and listened to the girls count to twenty, as they'd been instructed to at kindergarten, while they washed their hands with soap under the slow stream of water from the tap over the hand-basin. One of the downsides of relying on rainwater to supply the house was low water pressure, especially in late summer when the tank was less than half full.

After lunch, Jordan retired to the lounge with a beer, ostensibly to watch the cricket on TV, while Tessa super-vised the girls in the kitchen and cleaned up the mess they'd created over lunch. When she'd finished washing the dishes, she quietly opened the door and peered into the lounge room, where Jordan, who'd been up half the night keeping watch, was already slumped in his reclining armchair, fast asleep. Tessa closed the door as quietly as she could and shepherded the girls down to the toilet to empty their bladders, in preparation for the adventure she had in mind for their afternoon.

She checked her watch. Robbie had been gone for an hour and ten minutes. He'd be meeting his friends by now, she thought. That gave her at least an hour to make good their escape.

Robbie had taken her mobile phone from her, probably thinking that would be enough to stop her giving into any temptation she might feel about contacting the outside world. Tessa shook her head in disbelief. He was so sure of his hold over her that he hadn't bothered to take her car keys with him. Idiot, she thought.

With Jordan asleep in front of the TV, all she had to do was get the girls into her car in the implement shed and make a run for it without waking him. She'd already decided which way she'd go when she left the driveway. She had no intention of running into Robbie on the road if he came home earlier than expected.

'Come on girls, let's go and see if the chooks have left us any eggs,' said Tessa, slinging her bag over her shoulder and picking up the egg basket. 'Here, you carry the basket, Mia.'

The henhouse was behind the implement shed, where Tessa's Honda Civic was parked, with her travel bag of emergency supplies hidden inside one of the shopping bags behind the back seat. Access to the nesting area was through a hatch in the back wall of the shed next to where Tessa's car was parked.

As they entered the shed, Tessa looked back at the house.

The heavy curtains on the lounge room window were drawn, blocking sunlight from interfering with the screen of the TV and the view from the room into the shed.

Tessa opened the back door of the car.

'What are you doing, Mum?' said Mia.

'Put the basket down, sweetheart. We'll get the eggs when we come back.'

'Where are we going?'

'It's a surprise, now, come on, get in. You first, Ella.'

The girls climbed into the car and she buckled them into their seats, before looking over her shoulder back at the house. There was no sign of Jordan, who she hoped was still asleep or so engrossed in the cricket he wouldn't hear them leave.

She slipped into the car, thanked the Honda for its quite start, reversed out of the shed and then slowly made her way across the yard and up the driveway towards the road. At the first turn in the driveway, she checked in the rear-view mirror. There was still no sign of Jordan. She accelerated, turned onto the road in the direction of Balhannah, heading for the Police Station in Mt Barker.

She hoped she'd get through Balhannah onto Junction Road and to safety, well before Robbie was anywhere near Onkaparinga Valley Road and heading towards Balhannah from the direction of the freeway that connected the town to the city.

CHAPTER 14

THE MEMBERS of 4 Freedom gathered for meetings in the shed at the back of Jack Bragg's Semaphore home. From the outside, the shed looked like any of the other galvanised iron garages hiding in the yards behind older houses across the beachside suburb. Inside, however, it was a different matter. Jack had spent a small fortune creating his man cave. He'd lined the walls and ceiling with insulation and plasterboard, covered the concrete floor with slate tiles to conceal the location of his gun safe, and paid for the space to be connected to the electrical circuitry of his house so he could install a refrigerator and an air conditioner.

The refrigerator was kept stocked with beer. The gun safe, located beneath the Persian rug in the centre of the floor, held three unregistered semi-automatic rifles with their serial numbers removed, along with multiple boxes of ammunition, sourced from mates who didn't keep records or ask questions.

Robbie arrived at one-thirty on the dot. Jack didn't like to be surprised or kept waiting. As he climbed out of the Toyota across the street from Jack's house, he recognised a couple of the vehicles parked in the street as belonging to other members of the group. He hadn't expected those particular members to be at the meeting and wondered what their presence might mean.

He walked down the driveway past Jack's Ford Ranger and around to the side door of the shed.

'Here he is,' said Jack, when Robbie appeared in the open doorway of the shed.

'Jack,' said Robbie, stepping into the shed and nodding to the others.

'You know Alan and Ted, said Jack, 'and this is Alf. I don't think you've met him.'

Robbie had heard of Alf. He was a big shot in the movement from Victoria.

Alf shook hands with Robbie. There were no Covid protocols being observed here. 'I hear you're to be congratulated,' said Alf, releasing Robbie's hand. 'Everything going to plan?'

'The police have no idea who specifically is involved, if that's what you mean?'

'They spoken to you?' said Jack.

'They've spoken to all the parents with kids at the kindergarten,' said Robbie, 'and we had a visit from them this morning. They wanted to confirm where Tessa and I were living, since we didn't update our address when we lost our jobs.'

'How did that go?' said Alf.

'Couple of young constables, asked us where we'd been on Monday afternoon when they saw the Toyota.'

'And?' said Alf.

'Told them we'd been working on the farm.'

'What about detectives?' said Jack. 'Had any snooping around?'

'Some bloke named Travers called me. Wanted to know if I'd heard of a group called 4 Freedom.' Robbie smiled. 'Told them I hadn't.'

The others smirked at Robbie's denial.

'You weren't supposed to kill the mother,' said Alf. 'What happened?'

'She made a run for it with the kid. Hit her head when she went down in the yard,' said Robbie, deciding to keep the full story to himself. 'Anyway,' he shrugged, 'made it easier to get the kid. It happened. We couldn't undo it.'

'Use those number plates I gave you?' said Jack.

'Yeah.'

'Where are they now?'

'Buried them, like you said.'

'Where's the kid?' said Alf.

'At our place with Tessa and Jordan,' said Robbie. 'She's secure. She's not going anywhere.'

'Good,' said Alf, glancing at Jack. 'There's been a slight change of plan.'

Robbie didn't like the sound of that. He didn't like it when people shifted the goal posts after the game had started. 'What do you mean, a change of plan?'

'Don't worry, you'll still get your moment of glory,' said Jack, 'only a little sooner than we'd planned.'

Robbie looked at Jack and back to Alf. 'How much sooner?'

'Things have come into alignment earlier than we'd anticipated,' said Alf, 'which is why we're here.' He pointed to Ted and Alan. 'Look's like today's going to be your big day, Robbie. Are you up for it?'

Robbie smiled. 'You got that semi-automatic shooter for me?'

'You won't need that,' said Jack. 'You'll get better results with your hunting rifles, as long as you stick to the plan we discussed. One shooter high up in the storage shed and the others in the front windows of the house. That'll turn your front yard into a killing field.'

Robbie tried not to let his disappointment show. They'd promised him a semi-automatic and he'd imagined himself gunning down coppers Rambo style, not picking them off like a sniper, although he knew their rifles would be perfectly suited to that task. 'When do you want me to trigger the action?'

'How long will it take you to get home and get into position?' said Alf.

Robbie looked at his watch. It had taken him seventy-five minutes to reach Jack's house from the farm. 'If I leave before two, I'll be home by three-thirty at the latest,' said Robbie. 'Won't take us long to get into position. We're set to go.'

'I'll give Crime Stoppers a call at three-twenty,' said Jack. 'It'll probably take the cops a while to respond.'

'They could get to us from Mt Barker in around twenty minutes,' said Robbie. 'It'll take them a bit longer to get anyone up from the city.'

'They'll send someone out to check on our claim first, especially since they've already visited your place and received a friendly welcome,' said Alf. 'Remember to let someone survive your initial ambush so they can call for backup, which will give you a hell of a lot more targets for your final shootout.'

Robbie nodded. He'd been over the plan multiple times

with Jack and worked out how they'd conduct the initial ambush in detail with Jordan, who was a crack shot and never missed. Even Tessa was a good shot but, after her outburst that morning, he wasn't sure he'd be able to trust her with a rifle. He'd have to give that some thought on his way home.

'As soon as news of your ambush breaks, we'll move on our target,' said Alf. 'They'll know who we are and that we mean business after today.'

Each of the men hugged Robbie and wished him success with his mission. He in turn wished them well with their plan.

'If you're arrested,' said Jack, releasing Robbie from his embrace, 'we'll get you the best legal team money can buy. We can't let the bastards win!'

Robbie smiled at the irony of sovereign citizens planning to beat the system with lawyers. He knew Jack meant well but he had no intention of being arrested. This was going to be his moment in the spotlight, and he wasn't going to stuff it up. He was going out in a blaze of glory.

CHAPTER 15

DEREK HAD JUST FINISHED EATING the double-cut ham, cheese and tomato roll one of the team had thoughtfully decided to get him for lunch, when his phone rang.

'DI Ryan.'

'Derek, it's Harry Welcome from Mt Barker.'

Derek stopped brushing the last few crumbs from his bread roll off his lap. Harry was the Inspector in charge of the station at Mt Barker. It wasn't like they spoke every day, let alone twice in the one day. 'What's up, Harry?'

'I've got Tessa King and two little girls in my office, one of which is Ella Taylor.'

'Is she unharmed?'

'She's fine. She's sitting here with Tessa's daughter, Mia. Apparently they're friends from kindergarten.'

Okay, that's one of my worries solved, thought Derek. 'What's her story?'

'Short version is Ella was kidnapped by her husband and brother and held at their home outside Balhannah, the place you asked us to check out this morning.'

'Where are the others?' said Derek.

'King's meeting someone in the city called Jack, but she doesn't know where, and York's at home asleep in front of the TV. Or at least he was when she scampered with the kids.'

'What are you going to do?'

'I've already dispatched my tactical response squad to pick up York,' said Harry. 'If we're lucky, they'll nab him before he wakes up. Mrs King left the back door open and muted the alarm on his security system.'

'You know he's armed.'

'They're ready for that,' said Harry. 'She's told us they were planning an ambush.'

Of course they'd be ready, thought Derek. A tactical response squad had enough firepower to start a small war. 'What about King?' said Derek.

'We're hoping to pick him up on his way home.'

'Let me know how that goes. What are you doing with Mrs King and the girls?'

'I've got Liaison getting in contact with Dr Taylor and I'll hold Mrs King for now. You might want to send someone up to interview her while she's willing to talk.'

'You might want to call the Commissioner's Office, Harry.'

'I'll let you do that, Derek. I've got enough to worry about.'

Jordan awoke with a start. There was a loud gambling advertisement on the TV but that wasn't what had roused him. He'd heard a car door slam, and now thought he could hear the sound of pounding feet. Still groggy with sleep, he got to his feet to investigate and was half way across the room to the window when the door behind him burst open.

'Armed police! Put your hands up where I can see them!'

The light came on. Jordan turned to face the intruders, and raised his hands above his head when he saw the size of the weapon the officer was pointing at him. 'What the fuck do you think you're doing?'

'Jordan York, I'm arresting you for the abduction of Ella Taylor and the murder of Sarah Taylor,' said the policeman behind the black face mask in front of him.

A second officer moved in to handcuff Jordan while the first completed the mandatory words of warning dictated by the legal code.

'Get the fuck out of my house!' said Jordan, backing away from them. 'You fuckwits have no jurisdiction here!'

'We'll let a magistrate decide that,' said the first officer.

A third officer came in to assist his colleagues subdue Jordan. There was a brief struggle that ended when Jordan was handcuffed and dragged outside, before being locked in the back of a patrol car.

As the patrol car moved away from the house, Jordan's mobile phone started ringing. The officer sitting next to him extracted the phone from Jordan's pocket and looked at the caller ID.

'Who's Robbie K?' said the officer.

'Fuck you!'

The officer let the phone ring out.

CHAPTER 16

ROBBIE TOOK the Hanhdorf turnoff from the freeway and slowed to turn left onto Mt Barker Road at the roundabout. There was a police vehicle, a Toyota Hilux with a lock-up unit mounted behind the cabin, parked in among the vehicles in the car park of the Garden Supplies depot on the left, just past the roundabout. Robbie saw it and dismissed it. He was not exceeding the speed limit and had no intention of doing so.

He continued towards the roundabout at the intersection of Mt Barker and Onkaparinga Valley Roads, where he took the exit in the direction of Balhannah. He tried calling Jordan again. He still wasn't answering his phone. Robbie shook his head, the silly bugger had probably fallen asleep in front of the TV again. He wished he hadn't taken Tessa's phone with him but he had, so there was no way he could call her and tell her to lock the kids in the cellar. He'd just have to wait until he got home.

He looked at the time display on the dashboard. It was ten minutes after three. He'd made good time. Things would be hotting up soon. It wouldn't be long now before they were famous and people started to take their movement seriously.

As he left Verdun, he checked the rear-view mirror. In the distance, he could see the police Toyota trailing along behind him. He glanced at the speed reading on the dashboard. Nothing to worry about, he was under the speed limit.

Ten minutes later, he turned left at West Terrace in Balhannah and left again onto Greenhill Road. A couple of minutes later, he turned right onto Swamp Road. There was no sign of the police vehicle in his rear-view mirrors. He slowed when he spotted the mailbox at the top of the driveway into the York homestead and turned to make his way down through the trees into the yard between the house and its outbuildings.

Tessa's car was parked next to the tractor in the implement shed. He hoped she wouldn't give him any more grief about what he'd decided had to be done to advance their cause. He'd lock her in with the kids, if she did, and she could share their fate.

He opened the door of the Toyota and slipped out of the vehicle with practiced ease. As he closed the door, the police Toyota that had been following him appeared at the top of the driveway and a man, dressed head to foot in black and holding a large rifle directed at him, stepped out of the shadows of the interior of the implement shed.

'Armed police! Put your hands up where I can see them!'

Robbie turned towards the source of the voice, another black clad officer with a rifle standing on the verandah.

A gloved hand landed on Robbie's left shoulder. 'I said, put your hands up!'

Robbie spun and swung his fist at the officer, who simply

stepped sideways and then smashed him into the side of the Toyota.

'On the ground, dickhead!'

Robbie dropped to his knees. The officer pushed his torso to the ground, pulled his arms behind his back and cuffed him.

'Sit up!'

Robbie was hauled up into a sitting position and left leaning against the side of the Toyota.

'What did you do that for? I haven't done anything!'

'Save that for the magistrate,' said the officer. 'I'm arresting you for the abduction of Ella Taylor and the murder of Sarah Taylor. You do not have to say anything but, if you do, it may be used in evidence against you. Do you understand what I have just said?'

'You have no jurisdiction over me,' said Robbie. 'I don't consent to any of your so-called laws and you don't have my permission to be here or arrest me for anything. Now get these things off me and piss off!'

'Get up!, said the officer.

Robbie stayed where he was.

'Suit yourself,' said the officer, who went through his pockets and relieved him of his mobile phone, before stepping back to allow two of his colleagues to lift Robbie from the ground and unceremoniously dump him into the cage on the back of the police Toyota.

CHAPTER 17

Pat sat in a waiting area on the fourth floor of the Royal Adelaide Hospital. It felt like he'd been there forever. He looked at his watch. It was three o'clock. He'd been there since eleven forty-five waiting for news.

'Mr Travers?'

Pat looked up at a woman, too young to be a doctor in his estimation, who was wearing a name badge that clearly indicated she was indeed a doctor. 'Yes.'

'We've lost your father, I'm afraid. He had a series of coronary episodes after admission, following the one he had in the car. I'm sorry.'

Pat wondered what she really felt. He'd delivered that sort of bad news to too many people himself without feeling much emotion. He didn't feel much now, since he hadn't expected his father to make it.

The paramedic, who'd extracted his unconscious father from his wrecked car, had told him it looked like his father had suffered a heart attack, which explained why he'd driven his car through the rear wall of the garage, demolishing more than the brickwork in the process.

'What about my mother?' said Pat, remembering his father hadn't been the only casualty of his driving misadventure.

'She won't be in any state for you to see her until some time tomorrow,' said the doctor. 'She's been heavily sedated as part of the pain management treatment.'

'Will she survive?'

'Hard to say,' said the doctor. 'We'll need to wait for the swelling to go down and the X-ray results before we'll know for sure and, as I'm sure you're aware, she wasn't exactly in good health before this incident.'

'Right,' said Pat, thinking the doctor didn't know his mother, who was determined to live to be a hundred, despite her health issues.

'I suggest you go home and get some rest, Mr Travers. There's nothing you can do here. I'll have more to tell you if you come back around this time tomorrow.'

'Thanks,' said Pat, feeling somewhat deflated. He'd hoped to at least be allowed to see his mother before leaving.

'I'm really sorry about your father,' said the doctor, before turning and disappearing back inside the intensive care ward.

Pat's stomach rumbled. He realised he hadn't had anything to eat since breakfast. He set off for the food court on the third floor, where he knew he could purchase something to eat and get a half-decent cup of coffee.

As he sat at a table in the food court eating the meal he'd purchased, Pat's phone vibrated in his pocket. He pulled it out and looked at the caller ID.

'Hi, Derek.'

'Lina told me where I'd find you,' said Derek. 'How's it going?'

'The old man's gone,' said Pat. 'Heart attack. Several, in fact.'

'Sorry to hear that, mate. What about your mother?'

Pat took a deep breath and let it out. 'Hard to say. They won't let me see her until tomorrow, but at least there's some hope she'll pull through.'

'I'll keep her in my prayers,' said Derek. 'Thought I'd call and let you know there's no need to feel you need to rush back, mate, we've recovered the girl and arrested her kidnappers.'

'That was quick,' said Pat. 'Who were they?'

'That couple you were following up at Balhannah, and her brother. She got cold feet.'

'Is the girl okay?'

'Apparently, she's been reunited with her father, and the Commissioner's wrapped.'

'That's the best news I've had all day,' said Pat. 'Thanks for letting me know.'

Pat finished his lunch and decided it might be time to break the news about their grandparents to his own kids.

CHAPTER 18

D<small>EREK HAD JUST FINISHED TALKING</small> to Pat when Tim Healy approached his desk.

'Just had a weird call from Crime Stoppers, sir.'

'Go on.'

'They reported a call from a Jack Bragg, who introduced himself as the president of 4 Freedom, and then claimed he'd just found out that a couple of his members were behind the kidnapping of the girl we're looking for, and wanted us to know they were holding her at a farm that belongs to Jordan York outside Balhannah.'

'Did they get his details?' said Derek, wondering what this Jack Bragg was playing at.

'Captured his mobile number,' said Tim, 'but he declined to give any other details.'

'Follow up on that mobile,' said Derek. 'I'd like to have a chat with this Jack Bragg.'

'This 4 Freedom must be some kind of group beyond King and York,' said Tim.

'Maybe, Tim, or this guy was in on it with them and thinks he's triggering the ambush they had planned.'

'In that case, he's going to be disappointed when news gets out,' said Tim.

'Find him, Tim. We need to know who else is in this group and what they're up to.'

As DS Healy went to task someone with tracking down the mobile number Bragg had used, Derek called DCI Roberts. 'I think there may be more to this kidnapping then we suspect, sir. We've just had a call from someone claiming to be the president of 4 Freedom and telling us where Ella Taylor was being held.'

'This guy have a name?'

'Called himself Jack Bragg. We're trying to trace him through the mobile number he used.'

'You might want to float his name when you interview King and York and see what it gets you.'

CHAPTER 19

Saturday was turning into a long day for Derek Ryan. It was four-thirty in the afternoon by the time he and DC Palumbo arrived at Mt Barker, where Tessa King was waiting for them in an interview room.

He'd opted to take Lina with him to interview Tessa King, hoping her presence would encourage Tessa to talk.

Tessa King looked like a frightened rabbit caught in a car's headlights, thought Derek. Her soft blue eyes came up from the table as they entered the room and, then, immediately went back down to the table in front of her. She looked like she could use a decent feed and a good night's sleep. Her lank blond hair fell lifelessly onto her shoulders, and even Derek, whose wife complained about his lack of observation skills when it came to the state of her hair, could tell she hadn't visited a hairdresser for quite some time.

Sitting at the table next to her was the duty solicitor, a middle-aged woman with a world weary face without a smile.

Derek sat down opposite the solicitor to allow Lina to sit opposite Tessa, and activated the recording equipment, something he hadn't done in an interview room for years. Thankfully, the equipment hadn't changed all that much from the last time he'd found himself switching it on.

'Hello, Tessa,' said Lina. 'I'm Detective Constable Palumbo, but you can call me Lina. Okay? And, this is my boss, Detective Inspector Ryan.'

Tessa lifted her face and smiled at Lina.

'Would you like to tell us what happened?'

'It's a long story,' said Tessa, looking at her hands. 'Where's Mia? Is she okay?'

'She's with one of the Family Liaison Officers,' said Lina. 'They'll take good care of her.'

Tessa twisted her hands. 'I don't know where to start.'

'How about last Monday?' said Lina.

'Oh, it started a long time before that,' said Tessa. 'Even before I met Robbie.' She looked up at Lina. 'I feel so ashamed, so dirty and used.'

Lina reached across the table and held Tessa's hands. 'I see you, Tessa. I hear you.'

The solicitor pulled a tissue from the box on the table and dabbed at her eyes. Suspecting where this might be going, Derek was glad he'd asked Lina to take the lead with their questions.

'It started when I was little,' said Tessa. 'I was bullied at school. I was really shy and didn't have any friends, and Jordan bullied me at home. My parents didn't seem to notice. He did it mostly when he was supposed to be looking after me, but it got worse after I started high school.'

'How old were you then?' said Lina.

'Thirteen or fourteen when it got really bad. That was after Jordan left school and would have his mates over.' Tessa looked at Lina. 'I was scared of him. He told me he'd bash me if I didn't do what he wanted me to do.'

'And, what was that?' said Lina.

Derek glanced sideways at Lina. She seemed in control of her feelings. He braced himself, not wanting to hear Tessa's story of sexual abuse at the hands of her brother.

'Have sex with his mates,' said Tessa.

'How long did this go on for?' said Lina, maintaining eye contact with Tessa.

'Until I was eighteen,' said Lina, 'when our parents were killed in a car crash on the freeway. We had a big fight because I wanted to leave home. He hit me. I had a bruise on my face for weeks.'

'Did you leave?' said Lina.

Tessa shook her head. 'I didn't have any money and he needed my help to run the farm. We had a big talk after the fight and he stopped demanding I have sex with his mates. I worked as his housekeeper and general dogsbody until Robbie asked me to marry him.'

'When did you meet Robbie?' said Lina.

'He was one of Jordan's mates I'd had sex with when I was sixteen. He was the only one that showed any interest in me as a person. He joined the army after school, but came back looking for me when I was twenty-one. We got married on my twenty-second birthday and moved into a house in Stirling. He was driving a truck doing interstate haulage by then.'

'How did that work out?' said Lina. 'Was he good to you?'

Tessa smiled. 'Turned out he was like Jordan. He just wanted someone to look after him and be there when he wanted sex. At least he was away a lot and told me to get myself a job so I'd have something to do when he was away. That's when I got the job at the nursing home, but he wanted to control every thing. Even insisted we have that I will submit to my husband stuff in our marriage vows.'

'Did you get married in a church?' said Lina.

'Yeah, Robbie's family's very religious. He insisted, like he's done with everything else ever since.'

'What was it like after your daughter was born?' said Lina.

'Mia's the best thing that ever happened to us. Robbie is like a different person around her. He just adores her. At least I thought he did, until he told me what they were planning on doing after they'd kidnapped Ella.'

'Want to tell me about that?' said Lina.

'Jordan was the one that started it all,' said Tessa. 'Started sending us stuff about the vaccine being dangerous and taking Robbie to meetings down in the city whenever he was home. They were convinced the vaccine wasn't safe, and they convinced me not to have it. We lost our jobs.'

'Did you do your own research?' said Lina.

Tessa hung her head. 'I did what I was told, like I always do.'

'How did that lead to the kidnapping?'

'One of the mothers at the kindergarten mentioned that Sarah was the Police Commissioner's daughter. I told Robbie. He blamed the Police Commissioner for the vaccine mandate that cost us our jobs, when we'd exercised our democratic right not to have the vaccine forced on us.' Tessa shook her head and smiled, as if she'd said something she didn't agree with. 'The boys went to one of their meetings in the city, they're in this sovereign citizens group. Do you know who they are?'

'We've heard of them,' said Lina.

'Is this 4 Freedom?' said Derek.

'That's what they call themselves,' said Tessa.

'The name Jack Bragg mean anything to you, Mrs King?'

'He's a friend of Robbie's from his army days. I met him at one of the vaccine protests we went to down in Adelaide.'

'Would you recognise him if you saw him again?' said Derek.

'Be hard not to,' said Tessa. 'He's got a tattoo of a snake around his neck that goes up under his chin.'

Lina's eyes flickered briefly in Derek's direction, as if she wanted to know if he was going to ask a question. He nodded for her to continue, and told himself Pat had been right about her all along.

'Tells us about last Monday,' said Lina.

'Be careful, Mrs King' said the solicitor, 'you don't want to go incriminating yourself. You know you don't have to answer any of their questions if you don't want to.'

'I've got to tell somebody the truth,' said Tessa. 'It's not like they asked me if I wanted to be involved.'

'Tell us about it,' said Lina.

'They told me the plan was to get the vaccine mandate lifted so we could get our jobs back, and that nobody would get hurt.'

'What about Ella's mother, Sarah?' said Lina.

'Robbie said that was an accident. Said she tripped and hit her head. They thought she had just knocked herself out and were shocked when we heard she'd died on the radio.'

'You didn't think to report them then?'

'You don't understand,' said Tessa. 'I've lived all my life doing what other people have told me to do. I was scared of what would happen to me and Ella if I told anyone.'

'What changed?' said Derek. 'What brought you here today?'

'Last night I found out what their real plan was. They were going to tell you where to find Ella and ambush whoever turned up to rescue her. They didn't even ask me if I wanted to be a part of it. They just expected me to go along with their mad idea and get us all killed.'

'You did the right thing,' said Lina. 'They've been arrested without a shot being fired.'

'What will happen to me now?' said Tessa.

'That will depend on the Public Prosecutor,' said Derek, 'but for now, we'll take you and Mia into protective custody until we round up Jack Bragg and anybody else who might pose a threat to your safety.'

'Why would Jack Bragg be a threat to my safety?' said Tessa. 'He's Robbie's friend.'

'You ruined their plans, Mrs King, and I suspect that won't go down well with anyone belonging to 4 Freedom.'

'Oh, I thought I was just saving Mia and Ella,' said Tessa.

'You did,' said Lina, 'and now we're saving you.'

CHAPTER 20

ROBBIE KING WAS NOT HAPPY. No-one had explained to him what was happening after he'd been arrested and bundled into the cage on the back of the police Toyota that had followed him home from Verdun.

He'd arrived at the farm around the time Jack was supposed to call the cops and tell them where to find the girl, but the cops had been waiting for him. How had that happened? Had Jack double crossed him? He didn't know. He didn't know where Jordan or Tessa were either, or what had happened to the kids.

Robbie waited and listened. He couldn't see what they were doing but supposed they were searching the place looking for weapons and anything else they could find to use as evidence against him. He started to sweat. It was getting hot inside the box and his wrists hurt.

After twenty minutes or so, two constables got into the front of the Toyota and started the engine. The air conditioning came on and he felt a warm, then cool, stream of air on his face. At least they weren't going to let him cook on the way to wherever they were taking him.

He thought they'd take him to the Mt Barker lockup, but when they turned onto the freeway near Hahndorf realised they were taking him to Adelaide. He did his best to get comfortable for his second trip down through the hills to Adelaide for the day.

They took him to the City Watch-House, where he was processed. They ignored his protests and made him take off his belt and remove the laces from his track shoes, before pushing him into a holding cell and locking the door behind him.

The place stank like a sewer, and the stainless steel bunk was covered by a thin mattress of soft foam rubber that made little difference to its hardness. He realised the smell was coming from the open stainless steel toilet pan against the wall, but there was no way he could shut it out. The toilet had no seat or lid.

He sat on the bunk and waited. After about half an hour, a man of about Robbie's age, wearing a navy suit in need of a good press, appeared outside his cell.

'Mr King, I'm John Stokes, the duty solicitor. Seeing as you don't have a lawyer, I've been asked to attend your interview to look after your legal rights.'

'What legal rights would they be?' said Robbie.

'Your right to remain silent, your right not to answer questions beyond stating your name and address, and your right not to be tricked into saying something you might later regret.'

Robbie hadn't expected any help. 'Am I expected to pay for your services?'

'Only if you engage my services after this initial interview, and we can apply for legal aid funding if you meet the criteria.'

'And if I don't want a lawyer?'

'I'd advise against that, Mr King.'

'Fuck off!' said Robbie. 'I don't need you to tell me my rights. I know what my rights are! Now, go on, piss off!'

'As you wish, Mr King. I'll let the sergeant know your decision.'

Robbie turned his head away.

Ten minutes later, a constable entered his cell, cuffed him, and took him out of the holding area into an interview room, where he told him to sit. The constable stood by the door and they waited in silence.

With DI Ryan at Mt Barker interviewing Tessa King, the task of conducting the initial interviews with Robbie King and Jordan York at the Watch-House fell to Tim Healy. He decided to take DC Kevin Snow with him for support. There weren't too many situations Kevin hadn't encountered in his thirty years in the force, and Tim had heard about the crazy protests the prisoners had made from their arresting officers.

'Know anything about these sovereign citizens, Kev?' said Tim, as they made their way to the Watch-House.

'Bunch of bloody nutters who think they can pick and choose which laws apply to them.'

'Guess they'll be disappointed with us, then,' said Tim, as they entered the Watch-House.

The Watch-House duty sergeant caught Tim's attention as they headed towards the interview rooms. 'You here to see this King bloke, Tim?'

'Him, and then York when we're finished.'

'King's declined the duty solicitor,' said the duty sergeant. 'Told him to fuck off, in fact.'

'Could be an interesting session,' said Tim.

'Or a waste of time,' said the duty sergeant. 'He's in room three.'

'I understand you've declined the duty solicitor, Mr King. Do you want to call your own lawyer?' said Tim, as he sat opposite Robbie.

'Who the fuck are you?'

'I'm Detective Sergeant Healy, and this is my colleague, Detective Constable Snow.'

Robbie looked at DC Snow. 'You like taking orders from someone young enough to be your son, old man?'

'I'll ask the questions, Mr King,' said Tim. 'Now, do you want to call a lawyer or not?'

'I don't need a fucking lawyer,' said Robbie, 'I've got nothing to say that needs some smart-arse lawyer to work out what I mean.'

'Do you understand the charges you're facing, Mr King? Abduction and murder are serious offences that carry life sentences. Do you understand that?'

'You pricks have no right to charge me with anything,' said Robbie. 'You don't have any jurisdiction over me. Your laws don't apply to me!'

'You sure you don't want a lawyer, Mr King? I'm starting to think you don't appreciate the seriousness of the situation you're in.'

Robbie leant back in his chair and laughed. 'You have no idea what's going on, Detective Sergeant!'

'And, I suppose, you do,' said Tim.

'Too bloody right I know what's going on,' said Robbie, 'but I have no intention of explaining it to clowns like you two. You've already been sucked in by your overlords.'

'Be that as it may,' said Tim, wondering whether he should be requesting a psychiatric analysis of the prisoner before continuing, but deciding to press on and see how things went before going down that pathway. 'How about you tell us where you were last Monday afternoon?'

'I already told one of your goons I was at the farm all day with my brother-in-law, Jordon. Is he here, too? Have you arrested him as well?'

Tim ignored his questions. 'If you were home, as you claim, Mr King, how did Ella Taylor end up at the farm after she disappeared from her home on Monday?'

'Who says she did?'

'Your wife, for one,' said Tim. 'How do you think we knew where to find you?'

'You're lying,' said Robbie.

'I'm a police officer, Mr King. I don't tell lies in recorded interviews. It would cost me my job.'

'Then she's lying.'

'Want to tell us what happened to Sarah Taylor, Ella's mother?'

'How the fuck would I know,' said Robbie. 'I've never met her.'

'You take the car seat out of Mrs Taylor's car, Mr King? We've got the DNA profile of the person who did.'

'Good for you,' said Robbie.

'Remember that cheek swab you were forced to give us when you arrived here? We'll be testing it against that DNA profile.'

Tim watched for the slightest sign of a physical reaction and Robbie didn't disappoint him.

'Go your hardest, copper. You aren't going to pin anything on me, and even if you do, it'll be too late to make any difference.'

Tim glanced at Kevin.

'Know anything about a group called 4 Freedom?' said Kevin.

'No, old man, I don't.'

'What about a bloke by the name of Jack Bragg?'

'I know plenty of blokes called Jack,' said Robbie, 'but he's not one of them.'

'Pity,' said Tim. 'He seems to know you and what you've been up to. He even called Crime Stoppers to tell us all about you.'

'Bullshit!' said Robbie. 'You two are full of it.'

Tim looked at his watch. 'Interview terminated at nineteen ten. You can take Mr King back to his cell, Constable.'

'Is that it?' said Robbie.

'Don't worry, Mr King. You haven't heard the last from us just yet. We're just getting started.'

Jordan York was sitting in interview room four alongside John Stokes, the same duty solicitor Robbie King had dismissed with contempt, when DS Healy and DC Snow entered and took their seats on the opposite side of the table.

DC Snow activated the recording equipment and DS Healy went around the room confirming the names of those present.

'Do you understand the nature of the charges you're facing, Mr York?'

'I've explained the charges to Mr York,' said the duty solicitor. 'He's aware of the seriousness of the situation he's in.'

'Can you tell us how Ella Taylor ended up at your farm after disappearing from her home last Monday, Mr York?'

'Mr York has elected to exercise his right to not answer any of your questions, Sergeant,' said the duty solicitor.

'Is that correct, Mr York?'

'You heard what the man said.'

'Well, I guess we'll be seeing you in court, then, Mr York.'

DS Healy terminated the interview and called for the guard to escort the prisoner back to his cell.

When Jordan had been led from the room, DS Healy turned to the lawyer. 'He retaining your services, John?'

'No. He only wanted me here to back up his right to not answer your questions. Reckons he'll defend himself if you take him to court.'

'Did he tell you he was one of those sovereign citizens?'

'Yeah, but I told him that wouldn't wash with the courts, but he didn't want to know.' The lawyer picked up his things and made for the door. 'I might come along and watch if this goes to trial, Tim. Should be interesting.'

CHAPTER 21

DCI ROBERTS WATCHED the notification bubble announcing the arrival of an email arise out of the taskbar on his screen and then slide from view. He clicked on the email icon and opened his inbox. The Commissioner had sent him an mp3 file, attached to a short text message informing him the file contained a recording of a conversation he'd had with his grand-daughter shortly after she'd been returned to her family.

DCI Roberts opened the mp3 file and pressed the play button on his keyboard.

'Hello, Ella,' said a voice DCI Roberts recognised as the Commissioner's.

'Grandpa!'

That had to be Ella's voice, thought the DCI.

'Give me a hug!'

'You're not allowed to give hugs, Grandpa!'

DCI Roberts laughed to himself, as he imagined Ella reprimanding the Commissioner.

'Oh, I forgot,' said the Commissioner. 'I've missed you. Where have you been?'

'At Mia's house.'

'What did you do there?'

'We saw a snake! And, and we hid in the cellar!'

'That sounds exciting. How did you get to Mia's house? Did Daddy take you there?'

'Don't be silly, Grandpa. Daddy was at work. Mia's daddy and Uncle Jordan took me there.'

The recording ended.

DCI Roberts noted the Commissioner hadn't broached the subject of her mother with his grand-daughter, and wondered how they were going to handle breaking that news to a four-year-old. He was glad he wouldn't be the one doing it.

He decided to forward the email with its attached file to DI Ryan. There was no way the Commissioner would allow his grand-daughter to be cross-examined by a hostile defence lawyer, but the recording might serve as a useful corroboration of Tessa King's statement.

Out of the mouths of babes, thought DCI Roberts, as his email whooshed away to its destination across the spiderweb of cables and nodes making up the police email network.

Sunday morning. Derek Ryan sat at his desk reading the briefing report filed by the officer who'd overseen the search of the York farmhouse. He raised an eyebrow at the number of firearms and the quantity of ammunition found on the premises. Sufficient to sustain a considerable firefight, thought Derek. They'd been lucky. They'd escaped a blood-bath, thanks to Tessa King's warning.

He read the section describing the extensive security

system York had installed, including the note confirming the alarm connected to the sensor on the front gatepost had been muted, as Tessa had claimed. Clever girl, thought Derek. She'd thought through her escape plan before acting on it.

Next, he read the section about the recovery of the clothes and toys belonging to Ella Taylor, which Tessa King had told them she'd left in the bedroom Ella had shared with Mia on Friday night. The crime scene investigators had also confirmed that Ella had spent time in the cellar beneath the floor of the apple storage shed, where Tessa had told them she'd been kept in the days following her abduction.

All we need now is something placing York or Robbie King in the Taylor residence on the day Ella was abducted and her mother killed, thought Derek, otherwise there was a risk one of them would claim Tessa was the perpetrator, and not the hapless victim she'd made herself out to be. He wouldn't have that answer until Monday, at the earliest, but was convinced they had enough evidence to have York and King remanded in custody at their scheduled appearance in the Magistrates Court.

Derek looked out across the incident room. Most of the team hadn't come in yet, and some probably wouldn't be in until Monday, in any case. He hoped he'd get a quiet Sunday, so he could write up his notes in preparation for the meeting he'd secured with the Public Prosecutor's Office to discuss the case first thing in the morning.

He heard the ping that announced the arrival of an email in his inbox, and spent the next couple of minutes listening to the Commissioner's conversation with his grand-daughter. Too bad she's a four-year-old, he thought, closing the file and opening the case report template.

The telephone on his desk rang.

'We have a problem, Derek,' said DCI Roberts. 'These bloody 4 Freedom people have abducted the Chief Magistrate, and they're demanding an immediate stop to the prosecution of sovereign citizens and the passage of legislation guaranteeing their sovereign rights before they'll release her.'

Someone needs to tell these clowns how the political system works, thought Derek. 'How did we find out?'

'Their bloody spokesman, some clown called Jack Bragg, sent a video to the Channel Nine newsroom. The nerve of the bastard!' said DCI Roberts. 'Says if we try to arrest him, they'll execute the Chief Magistrate.'

'Jack Bragg,' said Derek. 'That's the name of the bloke who called in the details on York and King yesterday while they were being arrested.'

'Bastard was probably in on it from the start,' said DCI Roberts.

Having worked with DCI Roberts for years, Derek knew he hadn't called simply to discuss the news. 'What do you want me to do, sir?'

'Find the bastard and arrest him!' said DCI Roberts. 'Take him out, if you have to, Derek. We're not negotiating with these fuckwits!'

'What about the Chief Magistrate?'

'She can be replaced, Derek, but do your best to rescue her if you get the chance,' said DCI Roberts. 'There might be a few people in high places that won't look kindly on us if you don't.'

The DCI ended the call and Derek called DS Healy. The team's Sunday morning sleep-in had just ended.

CHAPTER 22

PAT HEARD the alarm sound and tapped the button on the screen of his phone with his finger to silence it. He was tempted to stay in bed, but while he'd been stuck at home with Covid he'd made a commitment to himself to lose ten kilos and increase his level of fitness.

Since his recovery, he'd been starting his day at five-thirty with a brisk five kilometre walk, followed by a thirty minute exercise regime, if he counted his rest breaks, and doing his best to consume less refined carbohydrates and red wine.

He'd read somewhere that you had to stick to a new routine for thirty days for it to become a habit. Seeing it was only day four, he rolled out of bed and headed for the ensuite. Ten minutes later, he walked out into the street dressed in his walking gear and headed off to complete the five kilometre circuit he'd mapped out on the surrounding streets.

While Pat walked, he couldn't stop his mind from thinking about the things he'd have to do as a result of the previous day's events. He was grateful his parents had gone to the trouble of arranging a pre-paid funeral plan, they'd even secured a double plot in Centennial Park. Well, double in the sense of depth. Pat wondered what his father would think of being buried beneath his mother. She'd always had the last word in every argument he'd ever heard them have, so he guessed her being on top would be a fitting way to end their relationship.

He'd contacted the funeral home on their after hours number when he'd got home from the hospital, once he'd found the copy of the paperwork his father had given him shortly after they'd entered into the arrangement. The funeral home had advised him they would collect his father's body from the hospital and meet with him at his convenience to go through the details.

He'd arranged to meet with them at the funeral parlour on Monday morning at ten, which left today free for him to start sorting out his mother's situation. Even if she hadn't been injured in the accident, she would have needed to be assessed for eligibility to enter a residential aged-care home following his father's death. She didn't have the mobility to live independently without him being there to do things for her.

She'd joked about moving in with Pat on the few occa-sions they'd discussed what she'd do if his father died, but that wasn't what he wanted. She'd drive him nuts. Fortu-nately, his father had been a member of one of the older government superannuation schemes, so she'd have the income to support herself in residential aged-care and, when they'd sold the house, she'd have more that enough money to cover the accommodation deposit she'd be required to pay.

As he turned for home, his thoughts turned to the case they'd been working on and he wondered how things had turned out following the arrests. He'd caught the coverage on the seven o'clock news, which had only mentioned Ella Taylor being found alive and two men being taken into custody at a farm outside Balhannah. He'd knew there'd be more details, but he'd have to wait until he was back in the office to learn what they were.

Fifty minutes after walking out the front door, he was back, feeling hot and sweaty, and in need of a drink of water. After quenching his thirst, he spread his exercise mat on the floor and worked his way through the low number of repetitions he could manage. It was a struggle, but he knew he'd get better with consistent practice. He'd done it before.

When he'd finished his exercises, he had a shower and then sat down for a breakfast of orange juice and poached eggs without toast. As he ate, he glanced around the kitchen and decided he'd better spend some time cleaning before he went to the hospital, otherwise his son, Alex, would be chastising him about his housework when he arrived to stay with him later that evening.

It was mid-afternoon by the time Pat arrived outside the intensive care ward where he'd left his mother the day before. Rose, his daughter, was already there, waiting for him to arrive for their appointment with the doctor.

'Hello, Dad. You look like an outlaw with that black mask.'

'Regulation issue,' said Pat. 'Haven't got around to getting myself some of those white ones. How are you, sweetheart?'

'I'm holding up, under the circumstances,' said Rose. 'Do you think Grandma will make it?'

'She's a tough old bird, but let's wait and see what the doctor has to say. How's Marty?'

'He's home getting ready for a school camp,' said Rose. 'He'll be away until Wednesday night. He sends his love.'

'Alex will be here tonight. He's staying with me.'

'Coming on his own?'

'Felicity's at sea. She's out stopping the boats,' said Pat, making air-quotes with his index fingers. Felicity, a communications officer on a Darwin based naval patrol boat tasked with turning boats back in the Timor Sea, was also a promising candidate for becoming Pat's daughter-in-law. She was the first woman Alex had seriously talked about marrying, so Pat was disappointed she wasn't coming down for the funeral with Alex. He'd enjoyed her company on his last visit to Darwin.

'Perhaps I'd better come over, then,' said Rose. 'We can have a family catch up. I haven't seen Alex in ages.'

'That would be good,' said Pat, watching the young doctor who'd spoken to him yesterday come out of the intensive care ward and walk towards them.

'Mr Travers,' said the doctor.

'This is my daughter, Rose,' said Pat.

'I'm Doctor Yeung,' said the doctor, facing Rose. 'I'm leading the team looking after your grandmother.'

'How is she?' said Rose. 'Will we be able to see her?'

'She's awake,' said the doctor, 'but she's heavily sedated, so she might not make much sense, but we can go in and see her, if you like?'

'What's her prognosis?' said Pat, as they headed into the intensive care ward.

'We will keep her here for the next few days,' said the doctor. 'She has a broken collar bone on the left side, where the seat belt cut into her, severe bruising to her chest and lower legs, and she's cracked three vertebrae in her spine. She was lucky not to have broken any ribs.'

Could have been a lot worse, thought Pat. His mother suffered from osteoporosis, in addition to the arthritis that limited her mobility, and his father had driven the car into the back wall of the garage at speed. She could have been crippled.

'Then we'll move her to a rehabilitation facility, most likely Hampstead, where they will help you work out the best options for her ongoing care,' said the doctor.

They stood at the side of the bed. Pat noticed the intra-venous drip and the screens displaying his mother's vital signs. It brought back memories of Pam's final days. He stuffed them back down into the dungeons of his mind where he preferred them to stay hidden.'

'I'll let you have a few minutes,' said the doctor.

'Hello, Grandma,' said Rose.

Mrs Travers opened her eyes for a brief moment. At least she'd recognised the sound of Rose's voice, thought Pat. He placed his hand gently on his mother's. 'Hello, Mum.'

His mother smiled but her eyes stayed closed. She was obviously away with the fairies and wouldn't be talking to them today. Best to leave her to rest, thought Pat.

'Come on, sweetheart, let's go and have a coffee and a chat downstairs. Not much point staying here.'

Rose leant over the bed and kissed her grandmother on the forehead. 'Love you, Grandma.'

CHAPTER 23

Her Honour Judge Margaret Rutherford, Chief Magistrate of South Australia, awoke with a start, surprised she'd slept at all. She'd tried to stay awake in the hope someone would come to her rescue but, since she was still in the same room, it was obvious no-one had. She wondered if anyone even knew she'd been abducted, let alone knew where she was being held captive.

In the dull glow of the light illuminating the room from a tiny window high in the wall above her head, she looked around her prison, and a prison it had been made to look. It was as if they'd studied the layout of a typical prison cell and constructed one to hold her in. The room was about the size of the small second bedroom in her apartment, but it only had the one small window, which she couldn't reach even when she stood on the single bed, on which she now sat with her feet resting on the bare concrete floor.

They'd taken her shoes and made her change out of her evening dress into an orange boiler suit. At least they'd let her keep her underwear. She wondered why they'd chosen an orange boiler suit. She'd only ever seen prisoners wearing them in American TV shows. Perhaps that was where they'd gotten their inspiration. She didn't know. All she knew was that she was being held hostage by a group calling itself Four Freedom, and they'd threatened to kill her if the police came looking for her.

In the corner of the room opposite the door with its prominent spy-hole, there was a stainless steel toilet next to a handbasin bolted to the wall, just like the ones she'd seen on her last tour of the City Watch-House. On closer inspection, she noticed her tiny bathroom had a tiled floor and there was a line of tiles on the wall behind the handbasin, something you wouldn't see in the Watch-House. It looked to the Chief Magistrate as if her captors had constructed her cell around an existing bathroom facility in the corner of a larger space.

These people are obviously making a point, she thought, as she crossed the small distance from the bed to the toilet in order to relieve the pressure in her bladder. I suppose I should be grateful they've at least given me a toilet and not left me to piss my pants, she thought, as she pulled up her knickers and did up the boiler suit before returning to sit on the bed. She looked at the spy-hole in the door and wondered if her captors were getting their kicks out of watching a sixty-three year old woman go to the toilet, and decided she didn't care even if they were.

She thought back to the events of the previous evening. She'd been to a festival performance at Her Majesty's Theatre in Grote Street with her long time friend, Mary Thomas. They'd enjoyed a coffee after the performance before she'd taken a taxi back to her apartment on King William Road, Hyde Park, just south of the city centre. There'd been two armed men, with their faces hidden behind black masks, waiting for her inside her apartment.

She had no idea how they'd managed to get around the security system, but they had.

They'd been polite enough, but insistent. She'd been intimidated by the weapons. She didn't like guns of any sort, especially those pointed at her. They'd taken her down the back stairs to the car park under the building and driven her away in her own car, using her remote to open the gate. Once they'd turned onto King William Road, the man sitting beside her had pulled a bag over her head and told her to keep her mouth shut.

The Chief Magistrate had no idea where she was, but she knew it had taken them nearly two hours to get there. They'd used a smartphone to record the video in which they'd threatened to kill her, and then made her change into the boiler suit, which had obviously been made to order. The fact it fit her like a glove made her realise her abduction had not been a random act.

Along with her handbag and her shoes, they'd taken her watch, before ushering her into the cell, which meant she had no real idea how long she'd slept or what time it was, except the light coming in from the window above her suggested it was now morning.

CHAPTER 24

SENDING the video to a newsroom had been the right idea, thought Jack, as he watched the news of the Chief Magistrate's abduction and the voicing of his demands spread across the mediascape. They'd made a mistake sending their previous demands to the police, who'd kept their demands secret and tried to get them to show their hand before they were ready.

They were ready now, though. He'd made sure of that, despite the shitshow he'd hoped York and King would create not coming off, thanks to King's wife betraying their plan to the police. She'd have to pay when he found out where they were keeping her, and he knew people inside the force who'd spill the beans on her whereabouts when he asked.

He looked at the screen displaying the view captured by the camera attached to the door of the room holding their prisoner. She was sitting on the bed looking at the wall in front of her. He wondered how she liked being locked up in a cell like the ones her magistrates sent his friends into for months or years on end.

Jack checked the screen monitoring the feed from the

camera at the front of the building. There was no sign of movement. He looked at the time display on his phone and decided he'd better do something about breakfast for his guest, who was still sitting on her bed in her personal prison at the far end of the shed.

He left the caravan he referred to as the command centre and climbed the steps into the one he called the bunkhouse to rouse Alan and Ted.

'Wakey-wakey, boys! We've got things to do!'

While his colleagues ambled over to the bathroom facilities of the little caravan park they'd constructed inside the shed, Jack started preparing breakfast in the kitchen annex attached to the caravan. He wondered how their prisoner liked her eggs and decided she'd get poached eggs on toast, like everybody else.

While he'd poached the eggs and waited for the toast to be ready for a coating of butter, Jack told Ted to invite their guest to join them for breakfast.

Margaret turned her head at the sound of the door opening. One of her captors stood in the doorway. He was unarmed, his face not hidden behind a mask. She didn't recognise him. He didn't look anything special or even intimidating.

'Breakfast,' he said, beckoning for her to follow him.

Margaret stepped out of the confines of her cell and found herself standing in a dimly lit shed about the size of a four court basketball stadium. There were two large caravans parked a short distance from where she stood. The annex of the caravan closest to her was well lit. She could see two men preparing a table for breakfast. Beyond the caravans, two

Ford Rangers and her Mercedes were parked in a line along the far wall.

She could smell freshly cooked toast. Her stomach rumbled. She followed the man across to the annex.

'Good morning, Your Honour,' said the man standing by the cooktop. 'Have a seat.'

Margaret did as instructed, suppressing her sense of repulsion at the sight of the dark tattoo of a serpent snaking around his neck. She'd never understood why anyone would want to do that to themselves.

The man smiled and slid a plate holding two poached eggs on toast across the table to her. 'Want sauce?'

'No, thank you.' She spied the salt and pepper shakers and helped herself.

'Eat up!' said the man, who'd obviously cooked her breakfast, as he turned his attention to lifting more eggs out of the pan on the cooktop and placing them onto the buttered toast on the other plates on the table.

Margaret felt somewhat out of place, being the only woman and the only one dressed in orange, as her three black clad companions joined her at the table and started eating.

'So, what precisely is going on?' said Margaret, cutting into the eggs and toast on her plate.

'We're giving your overlords an opportunity to correct their ways,' said the man who'd cooked her breakfast.

'In what way?' said Margaret, wondering who talked about overlords, apart from the characters in the fantasy novels she liked to read after a long day in court.

'We've asked them to stop prosecuting people like us and to pass legislation guaranteeing our sovereign rights.'

'But all legislation guarantees our sovereign rights as citizens,' said Margaret.

'Not if they don't recognise our jurisdiction,' said the man.

'Your jurisdiction?' said Margaret, finally understanding who she was dealing with. 'Jurisdiction is determined by the powers embedded in the constitution, you don't get to choose your own.'

'That's where you're wrong,' said the man. 'As sovereign citizens we get to say what laws apply to us. We get to choose how we're going to live our lives. We don't have to follow your rules.'

'I don't make the rules, I only apply the law,' said Margaret, knowing she was in a no-win situation. She'd dealt with people claiming to be sovereign citizens immune to the laws of the state in her courtroom on several occasions, and knew there was no way to reason with them. Even though they hadn't been able to prove they were immune to the law, as they'd claimed, they'd clearly demonstrated to her that they were immune to rational argument, despite thinking they knew enough about the law to represent themselves in court.

They ate in silence for a few moments.

Margaret thought she hadn't tasted eggs this good in a while. 'Where do you get your eggs?'

'We've got chooks out the back,' said the man who'd invited her to join them. 'There's nothing like fresh eggs for breakfast.'

Margaret smiled. He was right on that point. 'So, what's my role in this?'

'You're our bargaining chip. They give us what we want,

we give you back,' said the cook, who Margaret took to be the man in charge, since he was answering most of her questions.

These guys have no idea how the world of politics and power works, thought Margaret, or how easily she'd be sacrificed for the cause of maintaining law and order. These fellows might think she was someone important but, in the greater scheme of things, she was just the office holder of a position of power in the system, and the powers that be wouldn't compromise or negotiate to save her. They'd simply replace her and the system would continue. She looked directly at the cook. 'And, if they decide not to give you what you want?'

'We've played fair, so far,' said the cook. 'You've been treated fairly. After all, you're a political prisoner, not a criminal. But there are ways of getting them to see it's in their best interest to give us what we want.'

Margaret understood the implied threat but pushed on with her inquiry. 'And, if the police track you down. What then?'

'You'd better pray that doesn't happen, Your Honour, if you're planning on enjoying your retirement.'

Margaret finished eating her eggs. 'Any chance of a coffee?'

CHAPTER 25

DEREK SENT a uniformed patrol to confirm the Chief Magistrate had, in fact, been abducted, or to at least confirm she wasn't home. When they reported back to him that no-one was answering the door and that the Chief Magistrate's car was not in her parking spot, he told them to secure her residence as a crime scene and arranged for a team of crime scene investigators to attend the premises to see what they could find.

Then, he rang Protective Services to see if the Chief Magistrate was one of the state officials whose homes they monitored.

'She's on our list, Inspector,' said the officer who'd answered the phone at Protective Services.

'Any record of an issue with her system last night?'

'Give me a minute.'

Derek heard the sounds of a keyboard being used.

'Nothing out of the ordinary, sir. The system was armed at nineteen thirteen and then placed on standby at twenty-two hundred using the correct code.'

'Is the system on now?' said Derek, wondering if he'd

have to get them to switch it off when the crime scene investigators arrived.

'No, sir. It hasn't been armed since it was placed on standby last night.'

Derek thanked her and ended the call. He needed to find out where the Chief Magistrate had gone when she'd left home at thirteen minutes after seven, and confirm if she had, in fact, returned at ten o'clock on the dot.

He called DS Healy. 'Where are you, Tim?'

'I'm on my way in, sir. Should be there in ten.'

'Get on to the taxi companies and see if any of them had a fare either to or from the Chief Magistrate's residence in Hyde Park. I'll text you the address.'

After sending Tim the Chief Magistrate's address, Derek went into the incident room and spoke to DC John Cheshire, the first of his detectives to arrive for the day.

'John, get the registration details of the Chief Magistrate's private vehicle and then get on to Traffic for the footage from every traffic camera she'd have to pass going in any direction away from her place of residence between seven and midnight last night.'

When DC Kevin Snow arrived, Derek set him to work on backgrounding Jack Bragg.

'I want to know everything there is to know about him, Kevin. Find out where he lives, track his phone, go through his financials, find out who his friends are. If what Tessa King told us about him being in the army is right, he's probably armed, and if he had anything to do with what York and King were planning, he's more than likely looking for a fight and won't hesitate to carry out his threat to execute the Chief Magistrate once we get near him.'

'On it, boss,' said Kevin.

'Get the others to help you as they get in,' said Derek, hoping they'd get a break before Bragg carried out his threat.

Derek told himself to be patient. They'd find Bragg in due course and he'd pay for what he'd done. He went back into his office to work on the notes for his meeting with the Public Prosecutor about York and King. He noticed Lina had sent through her notes on the interview of Tessa King. He was about to open her report when his phone rang.

'Inspector, I've got an Associate Professor Thomas from the law faculty at the University of Adelaide on the line for you.'

Derek was curious. He didn't know any associate professors. 'Put him through.'

'The professor is a woman, sir.'

'Oh, thanks for the heads up.' Derek felt a flush of shame at being caught out in assuming the caller had to be a man.

'Is that Inspector Ryan?' said a female voice.

'Yes,' said Derek. 'How can I help you?'

'I just saw that terrible man on the news, the one who's holding Margaret, the Chief Magistrate, and I called my friend who works in your office. She told me you were in charge of the investigation.'

Derek wondered who her friend was. 'Is there something you want to tell me, Professor?'

'Oh, call me Mary, Inspector. I've been a friend of Margaret Rutherford since we were in law school. In fact, we were out at a festival performance last night. I thought you'd be interested in knowing her movements.'

'Very perceptive of you, Mary,' said Derek, hoping she

might provide the breakthrough they desperately needed. 'Where was this performance?'

'At Her Majesty's, in Grote Street. Do you know it?'

'Yes, I've been there a few times myself,' said Derek. 'What time did the performance end?'

'Around half-past ten, but we went for a coffee across the road so we could discuss the show before going home. We didn't leave there until after eleven.'

That was a good hour after someone had disarmed the alarm system in the Chief Magistrate's home, realised Derek. 'Did Margaret drive herself or take a cab?'

'She always uses a taxi when she comes into the city at night, Inspector. She has a private arrangement with a young Indian chappie, Randi something or rather. He drives for Suburban. He picked her up from Grote street after we'd had coffee. I saw her get into his taxi before I walked home. I live in the Rowland Apartments near the Central Markets.'

Very convenient for attending shows at Her Majesty's, thought Derek. 'Would anybody else know the code for her security system, Mary? Someone like a cleaner?'

'She has a cleaner,' said Mary. 'In fact, she uses the same service I do, Southern City Domestic Services. Do you want their number?'

'Yes, if you have it handy.'

Derek wrote the number onto the top sheet of the pad on his desk. 'Thank you, Mary, you've been most helpful.'

'I only hope it helps you find her, Inspector.'

Me too, thought Derek, as he ended the call and went out to talk with DS Healy, who he'd seen enter the incident room while he was on the phone.

'Tim, I've just had a call from one of the Chief Magistrate's friends. She said the Chief Magistrate took a Suburban taxi home from Grote Street, around eleven last night. The driver is a young Indian called Randi. Apparently she has some sort of arrangement with him.'

'I'll get onto Suburban,' said Tim. 'This Randi might have seen something when he dropped her off.'

'And, get someone to chase up Southern City Domestic Services and find out who her cleaner is. Somebody disarmed her alarm system using the correct code an hour before she left Grote Street. Sounds like an inside job.'

'Will do,' said Tim, casting about the room for a likely target.

'Sir,' said DC Snow. 'We could have a positive ID on Bragg. Someone's just called Crime Stoppers claiming they know who the man in the video is. He's given us an address in Semaphore.'

'Okay, Kevin, use that address to see what you can find out about him. I'll get Port Adelaide to send a team around to search the place. I doubt we're going to find him there. Find out what he's driving and who his phone provider is.'

'Right, sir.'

Derek rubbed his hands together. He now had two vital pieces of information provided by the force's most useful resource: the public. Soon, he'd know who let the kidnappers into the Chief Magistrate's residence and he'd have two ways of tracking Jack Bragg's movements.

He took a deep breath and went back into his office to read Lina's report and finish writing up his notes for his meeting with the Public Prosecutor.

CHAPTER 26

MONDAY MORNING. Pat sat at his laptop in the kitchen, scrolling through pages on the Internet researching the process he'd have to follow to get his mother into an aged-care residential facility. What had happened to the old-fashioned terminology of them being called nursing homes? He was following that thought when he was interrupted by the sound of his phone ringing. He looked at the caller ID: Lina Palumbo.

'Hi, Lina.'

'Hello, Pat. Just thought I'd touch base to make sure you're okay' said Lina. 'DI Ryan told me about your dad. I'm sorry it turned out like that.'

'At least he had no idea what he'd done,' said Pat. 'He never regained consciousness, which was probably just as well.'

'How about your mum?'

'She's not out of the woods yet,' said Pat, 'and, if she does pull through, I'm going to have to get her into a nursing home.'

'That could be tricky,' said Lina, 'given the pandemic.'

'I don't have much choice, I'm afraid. There's no way she can live on her own.'

'You could always move in with her, Pat.'

Pat heard the gentle tease in her voice. 'We're not all blessed with a mother like yours, Lina. She'd drive me nuts within a week.'

'And, how are you, Pat? That's really why I called.'

'I'll be alright, Lina. Alex is here with me. He's just gone for a run, and Rose is coming around for tea tonight. We'll manage.'

'You know you can always call me, Pat, if you need to talk.'

'Thanks,' said Pat. 'What are you working on now Ella Taylor's turned up?'

'You been watching the news, Pat?'

'No. Anything I should know about?'

'The Chief Magistrate's been abducted by 4 Freedom, the same group that claimed responsibility for kidnapping Ella. Only this time, they made their demands through Channel Nine. They got a video from a bloke calling himself Jack Bragg. He's threatened to kill her if we try to arrest him. You should check it out.'

'That name rings a bell,' said Pat. 'Can you describe him?'

'Thirty something with the tattoo of a snake on his neck. Lives down at Semaphore.'

'Does this tattoo wrap around his neck and go up under his chin, by any chance?' said Pat, recalling an image from his past.

'How did you know that if you haven't seen the video?' said Lina.

'Oh, I'll check the video,' said Pat, 'but I remember a Jack

Bragg from my time down at the Port. We busted him big time for growing marijuana. Him and his mate, Josh Handley. Handley had a property in the Barossa. We only caught them because we'd pulled them over for a booze bus and the stink coming out of the van they were driving was overpowering.' He chuckled at the memory. 'They both had that snake tattoo on their necks, but they'd be in their late fifties by now.'

'Perhaps we're dealing with his son,' said Lina.

'Be worth looking up the file,' said Pat. 'Might give you some associates to follow up. I think they both had young kids when they went inside.'

When Lina had gone, Pat sat thinking about the day they'd arrested Bragg and Handley. The clowns hadn't sealed the bags holding their illicit merchandise properly, and it had only taken a search of Handley's farm outside Lyndoch for the Drug Squad to discover where it had come from. Pat wondered what had happened to the farm. It hadn't been seized as the proceeds of crime at the time, since it had been in the Handley family's possession for generations. They could still own it for all he knew.

CHAPTER 27

MOMENTS before he was due to meet with Paul Webster from the Public Prosecutor's Office, Derek got the results of the comparison between Robbie King's DNA profile and the DNA profile extracted from the cells found in the drops of perspiration lifted from the seat in Sarah Taylor's vehicle. He smiled to himself as he printed the results, which placed King at the scene of Sarah's death. A death which the pathologist believed was a homicide.

'So, what do we have?' said Paul Webster, as he settled into the seat across from Derek.

'We have a statement from Tessa King detailing the abduction and the plans they had for ambushing our people when they went to rescue the girl,' said Derek.

'Is she willing to testify in court?'

'She's willing to testify in exchange for an offer of diminished responsibility,' said Derek. 'From what she's told us, it sounds like she was abused as a minor at the hands of her brother and subjected to coercive control by her husband, so she may not have been a willing participant in any of this, and she did come to us with the girl when she realised what their intentions really were.'

'I can't make any promises, Derek, but that's something I'll certainly take up with the DPP,' said Paul. 'What else have you got?'

'We've got video footage from a neighbour's CCTV showing a vehicle similar to York's in the vicinity of the victim's house on the day the girl was abducted and her mother murdered.'

'What's the evidence she was murdered?' said Paul.

Derek passed him the pathologist's report. 'She was involved in some sort of scuffle before she hit her head on that garden box. The fibres under her nails strongly suggest she fought back, and there's bruising on her chest indicating she was pushed, hard.'

'Have we crossed checked those fibres with the accused's clothing?'

'That's still ongoing,' said Derek. 'Our witness has told us what they were wearing, so we'll find it.'

'Anything else?'

Derek handed him the page with the DNA results printed on it. 'This just came through.'

'What is it?'

'It's the results from the comparison of King's DNA with the one constructed from the cells extracted from the perspiration lifted from the seat of the victim's vehicle,' said Derek. 'It confirms King was at the scene.'

'Does King know about this, or his lawyer?'

'Not yet,' said Derek, 'and King's decided to defend himself.'

'You mean he's going to swear at the magistrate and tell him he doesn't have jurisdiction, don't you?'

Derek nodded.

'What about York?'

'He's declined to answer any question and told us he'll be doing the same.'

'Bloody hell,' said Paul. 'Can't say I'm looking forward to the committal hearing.' He stood up. 'Is there anything else?'

'Have a listen to this,' said Derek. 'You won't be able to use it, but it corroborates what Mrs King told us about the abduction.' He played the recording the Commissioner had sent them of his conversation with his grand-daughter.

'Sweet kid,' said Paul, laughing. 'I can't imagine anybody else getting away with telling off the Commissioner like that.'

Lina sat in the gallery of the Magistrates Court and watched as Robbie King was escorted into the courtroom. He'd spent a couple of days in the Watch-House and appeared to be wearing the same clothes he'd had on when he was arrested.

The clerk read out the charges. The magistrate asked the prosecutor for a summary of the police evidence supporting the charge. Then he asked Robbie if he was being represented by a lawyer.

'I'm a sovereign citizen,' said Robbie, in a voice loud enough for Lina to sit up with a jolt. 'I represent myself!'

'Are you familiar with the laws pertaining to child abduction and homicide, Mr King?' said the magistrate.

'Your fucking laws don't apply to me!'

'Watch your language, Mr King, or I'll hold you in contempt!'

'Whatever that means,' said Robbie. 'When are you going to let me out of here?'

The magistrate slammed his gavel into the sound block on the bench. 'Order!'

Robbie mimicked the actions of the magistrate. The Sheriff's Officer stepped up beside him in anticipation of the magistrate's next order.

'How do you plead to the charges, Mr King?' said the Magistrate, ignoring Robbie's antics.

'You can shove your charges up your arse!' said Robbie, obviously pleased with himself and the ruckus he was causing.

'I'll take that as not guilty,' said the magistrate.

'Too bloody right, you will,' said Robbie, 'ya bloody great poof!'

'Mr King, I'm holding you in contempt and remanding you in custody to appear at a later date. And, Mr King, I strongly recommend you engage qualified legal counsel before you return to this court.'

The magistrate tapped his gavel on its sound block to indicate Robbie was dismissed. The Sheriff's Officer placed a hand on Robbie's arm and ushered him out of the room.

'Fuck the lot of you!' Robbie shouted, as he disappeared through the door that led down to the holding cells beneath the court.

Charming, thought Lina, as she waited to see how Jordan York would behave.

Jordan was led into the dock. No-one sat at the table reserved for his lawyer.

'Are you being represented by legal counsel, Mr York?' said the magistrate.

'Speak English,' said Jordan.

'Do you have a lawyer, Mr York?'

'Why would I need one of those?' said Jordan.

'Read out the charges,' said the magistrate, raising his eyebrows.

The clerk read from the charge sheet.

'Do you understand the charges, Mr York?'

'I'm not an idiot,' said Jordan.

'Yes or no?' said the magistrate.

'Yes,' said Jordan.

The magistrate then asked for a summary of the police evidence and listened while the prosecutor read from his notes.

'How do you plead, Mr York?'

'Insane,' said Jordan.

'I'll take that as not guilty by way of insanity,' said the magistrate. 'Has he been assessed by a psychiatrist, Mr Webster?'

'No, Your Honour.'

'Given the serious nature of the charges, Mr York, I'm remanding you in custody and directing that you be assessed by a qualified psychiatrist to determine if you're in a suitable mental state to stand trial.'

The magistrate struck the sound block with his gavel and the Sheriff's Officer led Jordan from the room.

Well, that was different, thought Lina, wondering whether York had decided on the insanity approach or was simply playing for time and hoping 4 Freedom's demands would be met. She didn't like his chances if he was relying on that outcome.

CHAPTER 28

AFTER THE COMMITTAL HEARINGS, Lina took a car and headed for the address DS Healy had given her for Southern City Domestic Services, an office on the second floor of a nondescript office block located on Greenhill Road, Parkside. It was almost midday when she arrived and searched the tenant board to confirm she was in the correct building.

There was no-one at reception. Lina rang the bell and waited.

An older woman with hair so black, it had to be from a bottle in Lina's assessment, appeared through a doorway behind the desk, holding a steaming mug of coffee. 'Help you, luv?'

Lina held up her ID. 'Detective Constable Palumbo. I understand you provide cleaning services to a Margaret Rutherford in Hyde Park.'

'I've been trying to contact her ever since I saw she'd been abducted,' said the woman.

'Contact who?' said Lina, sensing the woman's distress.

'Sally. Sally Gordon. She cleans the Chief Magistrate's

apartment,' said the woman, 'and she's not answering her phone.'

'Is that normal?' said Lina, thinking it probably wasn't.

'Oh, sometimes she forgets to turn it on,' said the woman, 'but I've had a call from the client she was supposed to be meeting this morning. She didn't turn up.'

'Is that unusual for her?'

'Sally's one of our most reliable cleaners. That's why she does the Chief Magistrate's place. I just don't know what's going on.'

'Have you sent anyone around to check on her?'

The woman shook her head. 'I'm here on my own on Mondays.'

'I'm investigating the abduction of the Chief Magistrate,' said Lina.

'What? You on your own?'

Lina smiled. 'No, I'm part of a team. I need to speak to Sally, so if you give me her details, I'll go around and see if she's okay and get her to call you.'

'Oh, would you? That would make me feel so much better.'

Sally Gordon lived in a narrow-fronted cottage in Young Street, Goodwood. Lina admired the neat rose garden at the front of the house as she walked to the door. There was no doorbell, so she knocked and waited. No-one answered.

She walked around the side of the house, past the older model Toyota Corolla parked under the carport, and looked over the gate in the low fence into the backyard. There was a fox terrier lying on its side on the stone path between the gate and the open back door of the cottage. The smell, and the spectacle of nature's scavengers in action, told Lina the little dog had been dead for some time.

She put her hand on her weapon and stepped over the gate. As she approached the partially open door, she slipped her hands into latex gloves, before pushing the door inwards. It opened into a small laundry. There was a load of washing in the machine and a small pile of clothes waiting to be washed on the floor.

'Sally, it's the police! Are you home?'

As Lina had expected, there was no response. She stepped over the clothes and opened the door into the house. When she stepped through the doorway, she found herself standing in a modest sized kitchen. It looked like it had been renovated in the not too distant past, certainly a few years before the pandemic had put a stop to such activity.

In contrast to the sleek modern appliances though, the floor was a mess of keys. There had to be at least twenty sets of keys, each with a coloured tag, scattered across the tiles between the refrigerator and the pantry cupboards. The keys Sally used to access the houses she cleaned, thought Lina, as she bent to read one of the tags. It had an address for a property in Parkside.

On the bench next to the sink lay an open notebook. Lina stepped over to the sink and glanced at the pages of the notebook. She saw names, addresses, access codes, and a ragged edge that suggested a page had been torn out. She thought she now knew how the abductors had gained entry into the Chief Magistrate's apartment, and wondered what price Sally Gordon had paid before giving up her secrets.

She pushed open the door leading out of the kitchen into the rest of the house, and found herself in a darkened corridor that stretched up to the front door of the cottage. The first room she looked into off the corridor was a sitting room, a room Sally would never again use for watching television.

Lina took a quick breath in as she made sense of the scene in front of her. The half-naked body of an older woman with short grey hair was lashed to a kitchen chair in the centre of the room. The blisters across the woman's chest told Lina she'd been tortured with something hot, probably the glowing tip of a cigarette, given the number of butts ground into the carpet behind the chair.

The markers of death that Lina could smell and see suggested Sally Gordon had been dead for as long as the fox terrier she'd encountered in the yard.

Lina went back into the kitchen, where she pulled out her phone and called in her discovery. Then, she secured the premises and waited for the crime scene investigators to arrive.

After she'd handed the crime scene over, Lina knocked on doors in Young Street. She'd have to wait for the pathologist to confirm a time of death, but sometime over the weekend seemed a fair assumption to Lina.

There was no-one home at the first house she tried, the one adjacent to Sally Gordon's driveway. The door of the house on the other side was answered by an elderly man wearing hearing aides.

'Did you hear anything out of the ordinary coming from your neighbour's place over the weekend?' said Lina, pointing to Sally's house.

'Not really,' said the man, 'but come to think of it, I haven't heard her bloody yappy dog for a couple of days.

'When was the last time you think you heard it?'

'Saturday morning, I think,' said the man. 'It usually goes berserk when we get home from the shops.'

'Do you drive or walk to the shops?' said Lina.

'Oh, it's too far to walk, especially with the shopping.'

'Have you seen any cars in the street over the weekend that aren't usually parked along here?'

The old man stroked his chin. 'Not then, but there was one of those big ute things parked in front of her place when we got back from Saturday night Mass. A big blue Ford. Nearly hit the bloody thing when I was turning into my driveway.'

'Did you see anybody get into that vehicle?'

'No, we went in to watch Death In Paradise. We don't like to miss it.'

'Was the ute still parked there on Sunday morning?'

'No, it wasn't there when I shut the front door around nine-thirty before we went to bed.'

Lina wrote down his details and explained why she was asking questions.

'Sally was a good woman. Wouldn't hurt a soul,' said the man. 'Why would anyone want to do that to her?'

'Have you heard about the abduction of the Chief Magistrate, Mr Kellaway?'

'Who hasn't? It's all over the news.'

'Sally was her cleaner, so this is probably related to that.'

'So, we're not in any danger?'

'I wouldn't think so, Mr Kellaway,' said Lina, giving him a card with her contact details on it. 'If you think of anything else, give me a call.'

CHAPTER 29

At four on Monday afternoon, DCI Roberts stood next to DI Ryan at the front of the incident room waiting for their team of investigators to settle.

'Locating the Chief Magistrate is our top priority,' said DCI Roberts. 'I want this Jack Bragg character found, people. So, who is he and where is he holed up?'

'What have you got, Kev?' said DI Ryan.

DC Snow opened an image on the screen at the front of the room. 'This is Jack Bragg. As you can see, he's got a distinctive tattoo on his neck that stretches around to the under side of his chin. He's thirty-five years old, spent nine years in the army. Trained as a sniper. Was discharged six years ago. Works as a security guard for N Group. Lives at Semaphore with long time girlfriend, Erica Bellows, who also works for N Group. Neither of them are known to us, but Bragg's father, also Jack, has a record as long as my arm, mostly for dealing but also a couple of aggravated assaults.' DC Snow turned the page in his notebook. 'Drives a Ford Ranger, S764BHJ. Mobile service with Telstra: 0418-578-210. Last location on network was in the vicinity of Hyde

Park, on Saturday at 23:15. Phone hasn't been on since. Last seen at his Semaphore address on Saturday afternoon, according to neighbours.'

'And, a self proclaimed sovereign citizen who's abducted the Chief Magistrate,' said DCI Roberts.

'Forensics are currently pulling his house apart,' said DI Ryan.

'Any sign of this girlfriend?' said DCI Roberts.

'No, sir,' said DC Snow. 'I spoke to HR at N Group. Neither of them turned up for work Saturday night.'

'So, she's possibly in it with him,' said DCI Roberts. 'We need a full background on both of them. Known associates, financials, the works.'

'Yes, sir,' said DC Snow.

'How did you get on with that taxi driver, Tim?' said DI Ryan.

'Spoke to a Randi Patel, who drives the Chief Magistrate into and out of the city most Saturday nights,' said DS Healy. 'Confirmed he took her into Her Majesty's on Saturday night around seven fifteen and picked her up from Grote Street at just after eleven. Dropped her home at eleven fifteen and watched her let herself in. Didn't notice anyone or anything unusual.'

'Okay, so that confirms what her friend Mary Thomas told me,' said DI Ryan, 'and Lina's found out how Bragg and whoever was with him got into her apartment.'

'They had the access code, a set of keys, and the code to shut down the security system,' said Lina, 'extracted from a woman named Sally Gordon, the Chief Magistrate's cleaner, before they killed her and her dog. And, one of the neighbours told me he'd seen a big Ford ute, a blue one, parked in front of the victim's house just before seven thirty on Saturday night. He didn't get the registration number.'

'Not Bragg's,' said DC Snow. 'Wrong colour. His is registered as red.'

'I'll let you know what Forensics turn up, Lina' said DI Ryan, 'but I want you, and DS Travers when he's back, to take the lead on that investigation.'

'Right, sir.'

'Any luck with Traffic, John?'

'Not yet, sir,' said DC Cheshire.

'Keep looking. Anything from Crime Stoppers, Tim?'

'Plenty of people confirming the obvious,' said DS Healy. 'Seems everybody knows who he is but no-one knows where he is.'

'See if we can find his vehicle as well, John. They had to get to her house in something.'

'Yes, sir,' said DC Cheshire.

'Right, let's get cracking, people,' said DCI Roberts. 'We have to find Bragg before he carries out his threat to execute the Chief Magistrate.'

CHAPTER 30

ON TUESDAY MORNING, Pat went back to work. He didn't
see any point in sitting around at home doing nothing. Alex
was catching up with friends while they waited for the days
to pass before his father's planned funeral on Friday. His
mother would be stuck in the hospital system for weeks. By
the time she was ready to be discharged they'd know the
outcome of her aged-care assessment and, hopefully, they'd
have somewhere for her to go. Work, Pat decided, would be a
useful distraction.

Once in the office, he logged into the administrative
system to update his attendance records and complete an
application for the periods of bereavement leave he'd taken
and planned to take. He was checking through his inbox
when Lina arrived.

'Wasn't expecting you back today, Pat. Everything okay?'

'Need something to take my mind off things,' said Pat.
'What are we working on?'

'DI Ryan wants us to take the lead on the Gordon
murder.'

'Saw that on the news last night,' said Pat.

'I'm the one that found the body,' said Lina. 'I'd say they tortured her to get her to hand over what she had.'

'And, what did she have?'

'The keys and the security code for the Chief Magistrate's apartment. That's how they got in. We know the system was put on standby more than an hour before she got home from the city that night.'

'How did they know this Sally Gordon was her cleaner?'

'That wouldn't be rocket science, Pat. Once they'd chosen their victim, all they had to do was watch and wait, and then follow Sally home.'

'These people worry me,' said Pat. 'They don't care if we know who they are. This Jack Bragg is in our face, wanting us to push him into killing the Chief Magistrate. He must know there's no way for his demands to be met. That would lead to anarchy. Every dickhead out there would be claiming to be a sovereign citizen outside the reach of the law.'

'You been talking to the DCI, Pat? That just about sums up what he told us.'

Pat shook his head. 'I know how the DCI thinks, Lina. Now, what have you established so far?'

'I'm waiting for the crime scene report and the pm's this morning at ten.'

'Speak to any of the neighbours?'

'The ones that were home yesterday.'

'Anything useful?'

'Large Blue Ford ute parked in front of the victim's premises around seven-thirty on Saturday night.'

'Get a number?'

'Not yet. Got a request in with Traffic, but we're in the queue behind the search for the Chief Magistrate's

Mercedes and Bragg's Ford Ranger, which we have numbers for.'

'Is it possible that was Bragg's ute outside her house?'

'Wrong colour but it could be another Ford Ranger.'

'Perhaps we can double check with your witness when we chase up the other neighbours.'

It had been a while since Pat had been in the Police Morgue, but it didn't take long for all of its familiar odours to seep into him. He glanced at Lina as they donned the required protective gear. She didn't appear fazed by their surroundings.

They went into the room where the post mortem examination of Sally Gordon's body was scheduled to take place at ten. The pathologist acknowledged their arrival and started on his examination, as if he'd been waiting for them to present themselves, which, of course, he had.

Pat watched, impassive, as the pathologist started his inspection at the head end of the body. He wondered what sort of life Sally Gordon had lived. She appeared to have been a woman in her fifties in good physical condition, prior to the events leading up to her death. Pat didn't know anyone who made their living by cleaning other people's houses, although he supposed there had to be lots of people, mostly women, doing precisely that. He'd thought about getting a cleaner after Pam's death but couldn't cope with the idea of a stranger being in his house while he was at work. Instead, he learnt to clean up after himself. Even his mother had been impressed on the few occasions his parents had visited him in his new house. Strange how they'd always expected him to come to them.

The sound of the pathologist's voice brought him back into the room, and he let that thought fade.

'Cause of death appears to be manual strangulation,' said the pathologist, pointing to the extensive bruising on the victim's neck. 'But there are signs she was tortured, using something sharp pointed and hot, possibly a lighted cigarette or something similar, prior to death.' He pointed to the row of burn marks on the victim's chest 'There are no other marks on her, apart from the bruising on her arms and legs caused by the rope used to tie her to the chair she was found in.'

'When do you think she was killed?' said Pat.

The pathologist stepped back from the body. 'Less than seventy-two hours ago, so probably sometime early Saturday night.'

'If she was killed Saturday night they were cutting it fine,' said Pat, as they made their way back to the squad room on the third floor. 'Must have been pretty sure they'd get what they wanted from her.'

'Probably explains why they killed her,' said Lina, 'so she couldn't raise the alarm.'

'They could have left her,' said Pat, thinking they were dealing with someone quite ruthless. 'After all, she was tied to a chair and lived on her own. The likelihood of her freeing herself and calling us before they'd snatched the Chief Magistrate seems pretty low to me. I reckon these guys like hurting people. They chose to kill her.'

'Do you think they'll kill the Chief Magistrate?'

Pat sat on his desk. 'Let's grab a coffee and then go see if any of the neighbours are home.'

'You didn't answer my question,' said Lina.

'What did Tessa King tell you about their plans?'

'Said they wanted to kill as many of us as they could and didn't care if they were killed in the process.'

'I think this 4 Freedom group is using this sovereign citizenship shit as a distraction. I think we're dealing with domestic terrorists with a very different agenda.'

'I'll take that as a yes,' said Lina. 'Do you think we should be talking to the DCI?'

'I think he knows the score, Lina. If I can see it, you can be sure he does.'

'Bit strange that they've told us who they are, don't you think?'

Pat got up from his desk. 'I think that's all part of their game plan. They want to give us a clear target to focus on, either as a honey trap, like they tried with young Ella, or as a distraction.'

'You mean their ultimate target is someone other than the Chief Magistrate?'

'They want to create chaos and we're just useful fools in their game. Come on, let's go get that coffee.'

CHAPTER 31

APART FROM MEALTIMES, which afforded her an opportunity to get some exercise, Margaret had been confined to her cell in the corner of what she understood to be a large shed. It had been quiet for most of the time, so quiet, in fact, she was convinced she was being held in a rural location. The sound of hens clucking in the distance during the daylight hours only reinforced her sense of rural isolation.

After returning to her cell following their evening meal, she'd meditated for an hour and then lay down on the bed and gone to sleep. There was nothing else to do in the semi-darkness of the weak moonlight illuminating her prison.

Margaret sat up, aroused from her slumber by the sound of vehicles, followed by the slamming of doors and loud male voices. She was in darkness and there were no windows she could peer through to work out what was going on in the world outside her cell. It sounded as if several others had arrived to join Jack and his mates.

The voices became subdued, suggesting the new arrivals had moved away from the vicinity of her cell. Margaret lay awake listening, wondering what the arrival of the newcomers meant. She waited expectantly, but nothing happened. Eventually, she lay down and stared into the darkness. Even the moon had vanished from the piece of sky visible through the tiny window high above her bed.

She must have drifted off to sleep, since the next thing she was aware of was the sound of the door opening, followed by the smells of breakfast cooking out in the vast interior of the shed. When she stepped out of her cell, there was a small army of men milling around the kitchen area waiting for a serve of eggs on toast. As she walked towards them the murmur of voices ceased as heads slowly turned to stare at her. She felt conspicuous, a bright orange flame in a sea of black.

'Morning, Your Honour,' said Jack. 'Sleep well?'

'What's going on?' said Margaret, spreading her arms with her palms facing outwards.

'Change of plans,' said Jack, indicating for her to sit. 'This is the Chief Magistrate, boys. Our guest of honour.' He placed her breakfast on the table in front of her. 'Enjoy that, Your Honour. That could very well be your last meal with us.'

Margaret looked up at Jack, as she picked up her cutlery and cut into her eggs on toast. 'You leaving?'

Jack smiled. 'No, but you are.'

Margaret felt uneasy. There was no warmth in his smile. She pondered the implications of his words as she ate her breakfast, doing her best not to let her feelings show and to ignore the men standing around studiously ignoring her.

After breakfast, Margaret was ushered back into her cell and locked in. Things had obviously changed with the arrival of the newcomers. She'd taken a quick headcount on her way back to her cell. There had to be at least twenty of them, all young men with bushranger beards, the sort she'd seen on TV acting violently at anti-vaccine mandate rallies across the country.

She sat on the edge of the bed and wondered what they had in store for her. Were they taking her somewhere else? Were they releasing her, or was Jack's meaning somewhat more sinister with his last meal reference?

She knew there was no point in getting her hopes up. When she'd first heard what their demands were she'd resigned herself to her likely fate, but that hadn't stopped her from engaging her captors in conversation in an attempt to explain to them the futility of what they were trying to achieve.

Jack had been impervious to her arguments, throwing all of her reasoning back at her as points supporting his view that the world was under the control of a ruling elite that didn't give a shit about the rights of ordinary people like them.

His companions had deferred to him whenever she'd tried to engage them in conversation, and she'd given up trying to persuade them they were making a mistake.

An hour after breakfast the door to her cell opened. A man wearing a black hood with holes for his eyes, an item of clothing that Margaret immediately recognised as an executor's hood, stood in the open doorway.

'It's time, Your Honour.'

The hooded man walked into her cell and grabbed her by the arms, forcing Margaret into a standing position. He pulled her arms behind her back and tied her wrists together with an electrical cable tie. The hard plastic bit into her wrists as he let her arms fall.

'What are you doing?'

'Carrying out the sentence of the court.'

'What court?'

The hooded man pushed Margaret ahead of him, guiding her out through the doorway into the interior of the shed. Beyond the caravans she could see a well lit area, where the men had gathered in rows facing a chair placed in front of the wall. To one side, Jack Bragg was standing behind a tablet computer mounted on a tripod.

The man pushed her again, propelling her in the direction of the chair. When they arrived at the chair he forced her to sit on it, before tying her to it with a black nylon rope. Then he stood behind her with his hands on her shoulders.

'Margaret Rutherford, you have been found guilty of being an instrument of the corrupt state of South Australia and sentenced to death!' said a voice from within the ranks of the black clad men in front of her.

'You're brave,' said Margaret. 'You haven't even got the balls to stand in front of me where I can see you!'

'You're nobody,' said the voice. 'Executioner, do your duty!'

Margaret felt something tighten around her throat, making it difficult for her to breathe. In a panic, she pushed against the rope restraining her in an attempt to fill her lungs, before losing consciousness.

CHAPTER 32

PAT AND LINA spent a couple of hours knocking on doors in the vicinity of Sally Gordon's house in Young Street, Goodwood. Mr Kellaway, who Lina had spoken to on the previous day, confirmed the blue ute was indeed a Ford Ranger after they'd shown him a photograph.

The woman living directly opposite Sally's house told them she'd seen two men get out of the ute, just before seven on Saturday evening, and enter Sally's driveway as she was leaving to meet her sister for dinner on Goodwood Road. There'd been no sign of the ute when she'd returned home around nine-thirty. Unfortunately, she couldn't give them much of a description, other than to say they looked like workmen and they both had beards.

No-one else in the neighbourhood had noticed or heard anything unusual.

'They must have gagged her before torturing her,' said Lina. 'I can't imagine her not screaming when they made those burns.'

'Bloody loyal cleaning lady,' said Pat. 'I would have just handed the stuff over or offered to let them in myself.'

'Makes you wonder, doesn't it?' said Lina. 'And, why did they kill the dog? It wasn't big enough to hurt them.'

'Small dog syndrome,' said Pat, 'a bit like small dick syndrome. All noise, no bite. Did you find out how it was killed?'

'Bullet through the head,' said Lina. 'They must have used a silencer, though, seeing nobody reckons they heard anything.'

'We're dealing with some serious thugs, then,' said Pat. 'It's not like you can buy a silencer on the open market these days. They've been prohibited for around ten years if my memory is right.'

'Only that long?' said Lina. 'Who could use them before that?'

'A lot of farmers used them.'

'So, it's possible there'd still be some out there,' said Lina.

'Yeah, if they weren't handed in when the law changed,' said Pat, 'but the penalty for having one is pretty stiff, something like ten thousand dollars or a couple of years inside.'

'So, we're probably not dealing with a couple of farm boys, then?'

'I wouldn't think, so.'

Tuesday's debriefing session started with an update from DS Healy.

'We've picked up the Chief Magistrate's car travelling north on Main North Road at Medindie, at 23:54 on Saturday night and tracked it heading towards Gawler, but there are limited cameras in that part of the state. The interesting thing is it was being followed by the vehicle registered to Jack Bragg.'

'Any sign of a blue Ford Ranger?' said Pat.

'Not yet,' said DC Cheshire.

'Get an alert out to the public,' said DI Ryan. 'We may get lucky now we know where to look.'

'At least there's a chance there would have been people out and about at that hour,' said DC Snow, 'even in Gawler.'

Although Gawler was considered part of the Greater Metropolitan Area, a lot of people, including DC Snow going by his comment, still considered it to be a country town, thought Pat.

'Let's hope so,' said DI Ryan. 'What have we got on Bragg?'

'I spoke to his manager at N Group,' said DC Snow. 'Reckons Bragg's a bit of a nutter, into conspiracy theories, QAnon and all that sort of stuff. Told his boss to get out of the city and set up a self-sufficient refuge in the hills. Something about society collapsing due to government overreach.'

'Any sign Bragg has followed his own advice?' said DI Ryan.

'His place at Semaphore looks like it's been locked up for a holiday,' said DS Healy. 'Obvious gaps in their wardrobes, not much in the pantry, and no devices left behind.'

'Where would he go?' said DI Ryan. 'Does he own anything up in the hills?'

'Perhaps he was planning on using the York place,' said DC Cheshire.

'Well, that fell through, didn't it?' said DS Healy. 'Who's he know up Gawler way?'

DCI Roberts threw open the door to his office and

stormed into the incident room. All heads turned in his direction.

'The bastards have killed the Chief Magistrate!'

'What?' said DI Ryan, turning to face the DCI.

'Put this on the screen,' said DCI Roberts, handing a USB stick to DS Healy. 'This just came through from Channel Nine. They got it ten minutes ago.'

All eyes watched the front of the room as a video recording of the Chief Magistrate being strangled to death by a hooded executioner filled the width of the big screen used for displaying recorded evidence. There was no sound until the end, when the screen went black and a voice they'd all heard before made an announcement.

'I warned you this would happen if you tried to find me. You didn't listen, so this is on you. Back off, agree to our demands, or someone else working for your corrupt government will be next!'

'Has that been broadcast?' said DI Ryan.

'No,' said DCI Roberts, 'at least, not yet, and we've asked them not to show it until it's been verified as authentic.'

'It's already on the web,' said DS Healy. 'Channel Nine isn't the only place they've sent it.'

'Do we know where these bastards are?' said DCI Roberts.

'Not yet,' said DI Ryan. 'We're having trouble identifying known associates apart from York and King, and they're not talking.'

'Do we have video of that anti-vaccine protest from December?' said Lina. 'Tessa King told us she met Jack Bragg at that rally. Perhaps we've got images of the people we need to talk to.'

'I'll find out,' said DS Healy.

'There's going to be a media shitstorm,' said DI Ryan.

'You let me worry about that,' said DCI Roberts. 'You concentrate on finding the bastards before they kill somebody else!'

CHAPTER 33

Margaret awoke with a start. Her neck hurt and her throat was dry. She was in a bed, a proper bed, in what looked like someone's bedroom. She heard a noise to her left and turned her head to see what it was. There was a young woman with a friendly face sitting on a chair next to the bed.

'I see you're awake,' said the woman. 'Here, drink this.' She held out a glass of clear liquid with a short straw in it.

Margaret took the glass and sucked on the straw. Her throat felt better. She sucked again. 'Who are you?'

'I'm Erica,' said the woman. 'I'll look after you.'

'What happened?' said Margaret. 'I thought they were going to kill me.'

'One of Jack's little jokes,' said Erica. 'You're already a sensation online.'

Margaret relaxed back into the pillow. She felt a hundred years old, not like an online sensation. 'Where am I?'

'Somewhere safe,' said Erica, taking the glass from Margaret's hand and placing it on the table next to her.

Margaret didn't feel safe. She wasn't in control of her

circumstances and hadn't been since she'd been abducted, but she didn't have the strength to fight, so she lay back in the bed and closed her eyes.

When she opened them again it was dark outside and there was a small lamp alight on the table next to the bed.

'Do you need to use the bathroom?' said Erica. 'You could probably do with a nice warm shower and a change of clothes.'

Margaret threw off the quilt. There was no sign of her orange boiler suit. She was in her underwear, the same underwear she'd had on since Saturday. 'A shower sounds like a good idea.'

'Here, let me help you,' said Erica, assisting her out of the bed. 'The bathroom's this way.'

When she'd dried herself after a long, hot shower, Margaret returned to the bedroom, where she found a clean set of underwear and a change of clothes she recognised as her own. Her survival had obviously been planned. She wondered what else they had in mind for her.

The door opened and Erica came in carrying a tray with a covered plate on it.

'Would you like a glass of wine?' said Erica, as she put the tray on the bedside table. 'I've just opened a nice Riesling.'

'Yes, thank you,' said Margaret, thinking Erica's service was a step up from what she'd experienced eating with the men. 'What's going to happen to me now?'

'You'll stay in the house with us,' said Erica, 'until the boys have had their fun.'

'Who's us?'

'Me and the Handleys,' said Erica. 'This is their place. Now, come on, eat up. You must be famished.'

CHAPTER 34

EARLY WEDNESDAY MORNING Pat was at his desk, drinking coffee and typing up his notes from the interviews they'd conducted the previous day, when Lina walked into the squad room.

'You get around to looking into that case involving Bragg senior I mentioned?'

'And good morning to you too, grumpy.' Lina sat at her desk. 'Not yet. Sort of got waylaid by Sally Gordon.'

'Okay, you stick with that. I'll get the file and see if it triggers anything.' Pat leant back in his chair. 'Sorry about that. Let me start again.' He smiled. 'Good morning. Hope you got a good night's sleep.'

'Did you?' said Lina. 'It's not like you to be this grumpy in the morning.'

'Might have had a few red wines too many,' said Pat. 'Alex is a bad influence on me.'

'Yeah, right,' said Lina. 'More like the other way round. How is he?'

'I think he's enjoying being away from home and

catching up with his mates,' said Pat. 'I'll miss him when he goes back.'

'You'll still have me to annoy,' said Lina.

Pat ignored her response and ran a search on the case database. He found the case file number and submitted a request to have the file pulled from the archive. Hopefully, he'd have the box to rummage through sometime tomorrow, if they could find it.

'Shit!' said Lina. 'You seen this?'

'What?'

'Someone firebombed the Chief Justice's place overnight.'

'Anyone hurt?'

'Don't think so. Looks like Justice Ditchfield put the fire out himself with a garden hose.'

Pat got up and looked over her shoulder. She was reading the overnight incident log. 'That wasn't on the news this morning.'

'Guess we're keeping it quiet,' said Lina.

'Well, if it was 4 Freedom, I guess we'll be hearing about it soon enough, especially if they recorded the fireball.'

Pat heard the ding that announced the arrival of an email in his inbox. He returned to his desk and found an email from Tim Healy. It contained links to several mp4 files and a request for them to review the video recordings from the December protest march Tessa King had spoken about. He forwarded the email to Lina.

'Tim's sent us some videos from the protest march. Let's see if we can spot Jack Bragg and highlight anyone who appears to be with him.'

They had four hours of video taken by several officers with different vantage points to work through and decided to split the recordings between them. Pat's head was swimming after half an hour of viewing.

'There's Tessa,' said Lina.

Pat paused his video and went to Lina's desk. 'Recognise anyone with her?'

'That's her husband, and that's Mia,' said Lina.

'And there's Jack Bragg,' said Pat. 'Stop it there.'

Lina paused the video and Pat looked at the faces of the men standing either side of Bragg. Only Bragg had a neck tattoo but one of the men looked vaguely familiar to Pat. 'I reckon I might know who that one is.'

'Want me to print this shot?'

'Yes, and let's see if we can find some details for young Handley. I don't remember his first name but he's a dead ringer for his father, Josh.'

'Where was his property again?' said Lina.

'Lyndoch. Run a search on Registrations for any Handleys with a Lyndoch address.'

Pat's phone rang.

'Better come up,' said DI Ryan. 'We've got a visitor from ASIO.'

'I gotta go upstairs,' said Pat. 'You keep looking.'

Pat joined DI Ryan and DS Healy in DCI Roberts' office. A man dressed in a neat grey suit, white shirt and dark blue tie came in with the DCI.

Pat had never met anyone from the Australian Security Intelligence Organisation before, at least as far as he knew. If this was one of their agents, he looked more like an insurance salesman than an intelligence operative to Pat.

'This is John Prentice from ASIO's counterterrorism unit,' said DCI Roberts. 'These are my senior investigators, John.' The DCI introduced his investigators in turn and then sat on his desk. 'John's got some intelligence to share with us.'

Pat took out his notebook.

'We have someone inside this 4 Freedom group you're dealing with, gentlemen. They've been on our radar for a while.'

His expression made Pat think he was feeling somewhat uncomfortable.

'Have to admit, though, we weren't expecting any of these abductions or the killing of your Chief Magistrate.'

'What were you expecting?' said DI Ryan.

'These people usually try to take control by overpowering local council meetings, but not this group. They've been posing as an anti-vaccination group, recruiting members during the lockdowns. You've probably seen some of the protests they've highjacked.'

'We've had some of our own,' said DCI Roberts.

'4 Freedom are a front for the sovereign citizen movement, led by a bloke from Ballarat called Alf Martin. He's ex-military. They've been recruiting heavily in the veterans community, especially among disaffected veterans with a beef against the system.'

'Are you saying we're dealing with a paramilitary group?' said DS Healy.

'Yes, Sergeant,' said John, 'and we've only just got word about what they're really up to.'

'Which is?' said DI Ryan.

'They're planning to seize the Barossa by force of arms and declare it a free state.'

'When?' said DCI Roberts.

'Saturday morning.'

The investigators assembled in the room looked at each other in stunned silence. Pat was the first to recover. 'How do you know this is going to happen?'

'We managed to infiltrate the group last year during one of their recruitment drives. We've got an operative inside their Victorian membership but we don't have anybody inside the local branch here, which is why their recent activities came as a bit of a surprise.'

'How reliable is this operative?' said DCI Roberts.

'He's one of our best,' said John.

'So, how are they going to pull this off?' said DI Ryan. 'The Barossa's a pretty big place.'

'It might be,' said John, 'but there are only three main towns. Their plan is to seize each of them by force and give the residents an ultimatum.'

'What, like ISIS?' said Pat.

'Precisely,' said John.

'But ISIS had an army,' said Pat.

'So does 4 Freedom. They have a hundred or so armed members, some of them are already in place.'

'Where?' said DI Ryan.

'They're gathering on a property outside Lyndoch and in caravan parks across the Barossa.'

'This property outside Lyndoch,' said Pat, 'wouldn't belong to a Josh Handley, would it?'

'How did you know that, Sergeant?'

'It's a long story,' said Pat, 'but I thought I recognised his son in a video taken at an anti-vaccination protest I was watching this morning.'

'What's their timeline?' said DCI Roberts.

'Our operative's reported members received final orders

this morning. They've been told to converge on the Barossa Valley and be ready for action by five-thirty on Saturday morning.'

'We'll need to set up road blocks at the borders and search vehicles coming in,' said DI Ryan.

'At least the pandemic's given us a model for doing that,' said DS Healy.

'We'll round up as many known members in other states as we can with the help of the AFP and local forces,' said John, 'but you'll have to neutralise those already here and stop any others crossing your borders.'

'Do we know where this Alf Martin is?' said Pat. 'Perhaps we can decapitate the organisation.'

'He's at that farm near Lyndoch,' said John. 'Apparently he's been over here since last weekend.'

'We need to set up a meeting with the STAR Group,' said DCI Roberts. 'We're going to need their firepower.'

CHAPTER 35

THE SPECIAL TASKS AND RESCUE GROUP had been established and equipped to conduct the type of operation DCI Roberts had in mind. Pat knew from previous encounters with the STAR Group that he and his fellow detectives would only get in the way of the highly trained and heavily armed officers of the taskforce when they went into action.

Pat made his way back down to the squad room on the third floor, more than happy to leave the planning of the operation DCI Roberts had in mind to the experts.

'What was your meeting about?' said Lina, as Pat sat down beside her.

'Briefing from some ASIO agent,' said Pat. 'Sounds like what happened to the Chief Magistrate was a bit of a sideshow to get our attention. These 4 Freedom clowns are apparently planning to set up a free state in the Barossa by force of arms.'

Lina looked at him. 'What?'

'According to our ASIO friend, there's more than a hundred of them,' said Pat. 'A lot of them are ex-military and they're armed.'

'How does this ASIO person know what they're planning?'

'They've got someone on the inside,' said Pat, 'who only got the word out to his handler this morning.'

'When's this supposed to happen?'

'Saturday morning.'

'Doesn't give us much time,' said Lina. 'Where are these people now?'

'Some of them are still interstate. The AFP is working with local forces to round them up but there's a group of them in the Barossa already. The DCI is working on a plan of action with the STAR Group.'

'What are we doing?' said Lina.

'Continuing with our investigation,' said Pat. 'They're not going to need us on the ground during the round up.'

'Thank God for that,' said Lina.

'Any luck with Registrations?'

'I've got a sedan, a ute, and a truck registered in the name of Josh Handley, and a blue Ford Ranger in the name of Edward Handley, who appears to be his son, going by his age. He's thirty-two.'

'Better give the registration number of that one to Traffic and ask them to narrow their search.'

'Already sent it,' said Lina.

'Okay, let's see if we can isolate anyone else on this video and find out who they are.'

Before leaving for the day, Pat read through the crime scene report from the Gordon murder scene again. He couldn't help but smile to himself. Her killers appeared to have taken sufficient precautions to prevent anyone from hearing them, but they hadn't been careful about hiding their identities. Apart from parking their vehicle in front of the victim's house, they'd left numerous fingerprints on surfaces in the victim's kitchen, and one of them had left a DNA sample on the discarded cigarette butts ground into the carpet behind the chair holding the victim's body.

Pat scratched his head. Whoever these guys were, they either thought they wouldn't be held to account or didn't care enough to take the steps required to make sure they weren't.

Given that Edward Handley was associated with Jack Bragg and drove a vehicle of the right make and colour, Pat wondered who the other person seen entering the house would turn out to be. He logged off, knowing he'd probably have to wait until everyone in 4 Freedom had been swabbed and fingerprinted before he'd find out.

CHAPTER 36

PAT WALKED down Angas Street to Victoria Square, where he boarded a tram heading in the direction of the Royal Adelaide Hospital. The tram was crowded with office workers taking advantage of the free ride to the railway station on North Terrace, as they headed home at the end of their day in the city. Probably would have been quicker to walk, thought Pat, as the tram driver waited for the lights to change before turning onto North Terrace.

The tram made better progress after its stop outside the railway station and Pat was soon walking up the path into the hospital. His mother had been moved out of intensive care to a general ward on the eighth floor, while she waited for a bed to become available at the Hampstead Rehabilitation Centre.

'How are you, Mum?'

Mrs Travers looked at him, a blank expression on her face. 'Who are you?'

'Doctor Who,' said Pat, sitting in the chair next to her bed.

'No you're not. He's much better looking than you.'

Her eyes smiled. Pat couldn't see the rest of her face.

'I thought I'd see you sooner than this.'

'I went into work. Beats sitting around doing nothing at home. So, how are you feeling?'

'Bloody terrible. Everything hurts. Someone has to take me to the toilet and help me have a shower.'

'They giving you something for the pain?'

'Nurse comes around every four hours. They even wake me up in the middle of the night.'

Pat gathered from the whine in her voice that she wasn't happy about that. 'I guess that's better than waking up in pain.'

'I suppose, but I'd rather they let me sleep.'

'Won't be forever, Mum.'

'How long are they keeping me here? No-one tells me anything.'

Pat doubted that was true but knew better than to dispute his mother's version of events. 'They're waiting on a bed at Hampstead.'

'What, waiting for some other poor bugger to die so I can have her bed?'

'Waiting for someone to be well enough to go home, I'd say. It's a rehabilitation centre, not a palliative care unit.'

'Can you pass me that glass with the straw in it?'

Pat waited while she emptied the glass, before giving it back to him.

'Can you top it up from the jug?'

Pat replenished the glass with what looked like water from the jug on her bedside cabinet and wondered what it really contained.

'When will I be going home?'

Pat sat back in his chair. He'd known the question would

come up and wasn't looking forward to the conversation they were about to have. 'You probably won't be going home, Mum.'

'I don't see why not,' said Mrs Travers.

'Mum, you can't look after yourself.'

'Of course I can!'

Pat took a deep breath. She was doing exactly what he'd thought she do. Insist on being able to take care of herself, even though his father had been doing everything for her for the last few years.

'When was the last time you cooked a meal or did the shopping on your own?'

'Just because I let your father do things for me doesn't mean I can't do them for myself.'

'You can't even make your bed let alone change the sheets.'

'You can do that for me.'

'I'm not always around, Mum. Remember when I was away last year? Sometimes I can be away for weeks.'

'I'll call Rose if I have to. I'm sure she'd do that for me if you weren't around.'

Pat closed his eyes. Her mind still worked, even though her body had started withdrawing services from her conscious control.

'And, what if you have a fall?

'I'll call one of the neighbours or the ambulance.'

'What if you can't get to the phone or break something?'

'I'm not that fragile!'

'Mum, you've got osteoporosis. That's medical speak for having fragile bones. You're lucky you only broke your collar bone and cracked three vertebrae.'

'Well, I won't be driving. They took away my licence.'

Interesting deflection, thought Pat. 'And, why was that?'

'The silly man failed me. Said I didn't know the road rules.'

Pat smiled. He'd heard that line before. 'He failed you because your reaction times are too slow and you don't have the strength in your arms to control a car.'

'How do you know that? Have you been checking up on me?'

'Dad showed me the letter.'

'Traitor. Never could keep a secret!'

'That might be true, Mum, but he's not here to help you anymore.'

His mother turned her head and fixed her gaze on him. 'You realise he tried to kill us, don't you?'

'What?'

'He did it on purpose.'

'You mean driving into the wall?'

'He wanted to end it.'

Pat leant towards his mother and took her hands in his. 'He had a heart attack, Mum. He had no idea what he was doing.'

'Oh, rubbish! He told me he'd had enough.'

'When was this?' said Pat.

'When we got in the car at the supermarket. He was cross with me.'

'That doesn't mean he wanted to kill you, Mum.' But it might have stressed him out enough to blow a fuse in his heart, thought Pat. 'He loved you.'

'Love? Don't give me that rubbish! Your father only stayed with me because no-one else would have him. You've no idea what I put up with.'

Pat had heard this story before, too. Whenever his

mother was angry with his father she'd trot out a litany of his sins, real and imagined. Pat knew his father hadn't been a saint, but the man hadn't been a hopeless sinner either. In fact, he'd been devoted to her as far as Pat could tell.

'What have you decided about the funeral?'

'It's out of the question. I can hardly stand lying in this bed. It nearly kills me when I sit in the chair. I'm not coming!'

'Fair enough. They're going to stream the service. Do you want me to send you the link?'

'You can take me to the cemetery when I get out of here. That will be enough.'

'If that's what you want.'

'What I want is to go home.'

Here we go again, thought Pat. 'The doctors will arrange for someone to assess if you can go home when you're at Hampstead.'

'Why can't I just go home?'

'Mum, they need to assess whether you're eligible for an assisted living package, so you can get help to live at home, or whether you need to go into residential care where there will be people to look after you all the time.'

'You're just like your father. You just want to get rid of me!'

An orderly entered the room and placed a tray on the table with his mother's dinner on it.

Pat lifted the cover from the plate. 'I see you haven't lost your appetite.'

'Bloody stuff is disgusting. They can't even cook an egg properly, but I have to eat something.'

Pat helped his mother rearrange her pillows and raise the bed so she could reach her dinner.

'You got any washing that needs doing?'

Mrs Travers pointed to the wardrobe in the corner of the room. 'It's in a bag on the bottom of that cupboard over there.'

Pat retrieved his mother's bag of soiled knickers and nightgowns. 'I'll bring in some fresh stuff tomorrow. Enjoy your dinner.'

'Say hello to Rose and Alex for me.'

Pat kissed his mother on the forehead through his face mask and headed for the exit.

It was seven-twenty when Pat got home. Alex was watching the news.

'Just let me throw this stuff in the washing machine.'

'What are you washing now, Dad?'

'Your grandmother's underwear and nighties.'

'Gee, Dad. Didn't know you were so domesticated.'

'Someone has to do it. Won't be a minute.'

Pat set the dial to delicates, threw in his mother's dirty laundry, closed the door, added a scoop of detergent into the drawer, and pressed the button that switched on the washing machine.

'That should be done by the time we get back. Come on, let's go. I could eat a horse.'

'Thought you were cutting down.'

'Stop being so bloody literal.'

They walked down the street to the hotel on the corner, which had become one of Pat's regular eating places since he'd moved across town to avoid the establishments he'd frequented with Pam. The place served decent food and was only minutes from home. What more could he ask?

They ordered the porterhouse and a bottle of red, Pat opting for the smaller size steak.

'You making any progress on that case you're working on?'

'We had a bit of a breakthrough today,' said Pat.

'Didn't see anything on the news.'

'It won't be on the news, mate. Not until it's over.'

Alex raised an eyebrow.

'Can't say any more.'

'What about the Chief Justice being firebombed? Has someone got it in for the courts down here?'

The waiter arrived with their bottle of Shiraz and poured wine into their glasses. 'Enjoy.'

Pat let his wine stand to give it a chance to breathe. 'Ever heard of sovereign citizens?'

'Read something about them online.'

'They're trying to get our attention.'

'Why?'

'They want a law passed exempting them from the law.'

Alex laughed. 'That's a bit bizarre, isn't it?'

'Their whole movement's a bit bizarre, if you ask me,' said Pat, taking a sip of his wine. 'Usually they claim they're exempt from any laws passed in Australia because, according to them, Australia is not a legitimate state. This lot seem to be trying to get the government to recognise their claim to being outside the reach of the law.'

'Most of the stuff online seems to be about groups in the States.'

'I think you'll find they're everywhere,' said Pat.

Their steaks arrived, along with the promised bowl of garden salad.

Alex used the tongs to transfer a serve of salad onto his plate and pushed the bowl towards Pat. 'How was grandma?'

Pat served himself some of the salad and started on the steak. 'You should go in and see her.'

'I might do that. I've got nothing on tomorrow.'

'Don't tell her that. Let her think you've made an effort to see her while you're home.'

'Is she coming to the funeral service?'

'Nah, she hasn't forgiven your grandfather for trying to kill her.'

'You're joking, aren't you?'

'Wish I was,' said Pat. 'I had to sit through another round of her he never loved me routine.'

'Some things never change.'

Pat stopped eating. 'Promise me you'll tell me if I start sounding like her.'

'Don't worry, Dad. I reckon you took after Grandpa.'

'Thanks. Speaking of grandfathers, when are you planning on making me one?'

'I'm deferring to big sister on that one, Dad,' said Alex. 'She's already taken the plunge into marriage. We haven't made it that far yet.'

'Yeah, just don't wait forever, mate. Kids are easier to juggle when you're young.'

'We're talking about it.'

'Takes more than talking, son, or did I forget to give you that talk?'

Alex laughed. 'What about you, Dad. It's been more than five years since Mum died.'

Pat took another sip of his wine. 'Haven't met anyone yet.'

'Are you looking? Seriously?'

Pat shook his head. 'Not really.'

'What about this Lina at work? You seemed pretty taken with her when you were last up.'

Pat smiled. 'Mate, she's your age. You'll get to meet her on Friday. She says she's coming to the funeral. If I were twenty years younger, maybe I'd have a chance, but let's not go there.'

'So, she's your type then?'

'She's just not old enough,' said Pat. 'I'm not sure I want to be making out with a younger woman.'

'You'd need to lose a bit of weight, Dad.'

'Yeah, and get fit. I'm struggling to pass the physical at work, which is pretty basic. Doubt I could keep up with a young lover.'

'Motivation,' said Alex.

'Stop it!'

'You started it with your wanting to be a grandfather question.'

'I was only joshing with you, mate. You and Felicity getting married and having kids is really none of my business. You need to live your own life, not my dreams.'

'It's okay, Dad. Want a top up?'

CHAPTER 37

MARGARET WAS SITTING on the verandah of the house with Erica, where they'd eaten breakfast in the cool morning air. She heard the helicopter before she saw it. It was quite high in the sky.

The noise became louder as it approached and passed overhead, before continuing on its way without stopping. She thought it looked like the police helicopter and wondered where it was going. It would hardly be looking for her, since, as far as the world knew, she was dead.

She noticed several men standing in the yard looking up at the disappearing helicopter, some of them through binoculars. When the helicopter didn't veer from its course, the men shrugged and went back to their tents.

'Want another coffee?' said Erica.

'That would be nice.'

While Erica fussed over the coffees, Margaret ran her eyes over the field of tents and parked vehicles that had sprung up beside the shed in which she'd previously been confined. There had to be around fifty people camping in and around the shed. There was even a bank of portable toilets, like the ones she'd seen at outside event venues, installed along one side of the shed.

When she'd asked Erica what was going on, she'd explained that Jack was running a program to help some of his army mates reintegrate back into civilian life. They certainly looked like what Margaret imagined soldiers to be: huge, and exuding masculine energy.

She hadn't been inside the shed since the morning of her execution, so she had no real idea what the men were doing when gathered in there. All she knew was she was being treated as a house guest by Erica and the Handleys, despite being their prisoner. She had freedom of movement inside the house and gardens, but not beyond. There was always a man at the gate. A man with a gun.

Twenty minutes later, after she'd finished her second coffee, the helicopter came back. It was much lower this time, the police markings on its fuselage clearly visible from her vantage point. The reverberations from its thudding rotor blades rattled the empty breakfast dishes on the table as it swept over the homestead, before turning south and disappearing into the distance. As on its previous pass, she noticed a couple of the men watch it fly over through binoculars, before returning to whatever it was they were doing in the shed.

CHAPTER 38

ON THURSDAY MORNING, Pat and Lina started their shift following up leads from the public on the images from the video of the protest march they'd released to the media. Several callers had identified one of the men standing with Jack Bragg as Alan Broderick, a resident of Largs North. One caller had rung in to inform them that the individual standing behind Broderick, who they'd already identified as Edward Handley, was known on the street as Ted.

Lina searched Registrations for details on Broderick.

'Got an Alan Broderick in Woodhall Road.'

'Got a mobile number?'

'Yes.'

Pat keyed the number into the phone tracking system, and hit enter. 'Looks like our Mr Broderick is in the vicinity of Lyndoch.'

'Guess we won't be going to see him today. Where was he Saturday night?'

Pat scrolled through the rows of location data on his screen. 'He was in Goodwood around seven.'

'Anywhere near Young Street?'

Pat opened the map showing the location of the tower Broderick's phone had pinged. 'Yep.'

'Not as smart as Handley, then,' said Lina. 'At least he had the sense to turn his phone off.'

'Let's see if he's switched it back on.' Pat looked through his notes and keyed in Handley's number. 'Bingo! He's with Broderick.'

'Be good if we could confirm that Ranger parked in front of Sally Gordon's on Saturday was Handley's.'

'Give John Cheshire a call and see if he's had any luck with Traffic.'

While Lina spoke to DC Cheshire, Pat read through the crime scene report from the Chief Justice's firebombing. It read more like an account of a nuisance attack than anything more serious. The offender had thrown a Molotov cocktail at the front door of the house and run.

Although the episode had been recorded by the Chief Justice's security camera, they had little of any real value to go on. The attacker appeared to be a young man wearing a hoody and a face mask, who'd known enough about forensics to have wiped down the bottle before throwing it up against the door.

Pat heard Lina end her call. 'Any luck?'

'They've got it on Greenhill Road, Goodwood, at 20:13 and again on Port Road, Hindmarsh, around fifteen minutes later, heading towards the Port.'

'Guess they could have been heading to Bragg's at Semaphore.'

'John's trying to track it but we don't have cameras everywhere.'

Pat's phone buzzed. He looked at the message. 'I'm wanted upstairs.'

Pat joined Tim Healy and Derek Ryan in DCI Roberts' office.

'STAR Group conducted a reconnaissance flight across the Barossa this morning and they've had Nuriootpa quietly checking on recent arrivals at caravan parks in and around the valley,' said DCI Roberts. 'Good news is the Handley farm outside Lyndoch appears to be their main campsite.'

'What's the plan?' said Derek.

'ASIO's mole has told them they've been given three gathering points for Saturday morning, one in each of Tanunda, Nuriootpa, and Angaston. We're hoping to round most of them up before Saturday.'

'When?'

'All happening first thing tomorrow.'

'Dawn raids?'

'That, and check points on all main roads into the Barossa. Hopefully, once word gets out we've neutralised their main party, any stragglers will have second thoughts and go home.'

'Let's hope they have the good sense to give up without starting a war,' said Tim.

DCI Roberts smiled. 'I'm sure STAR Group are up for the fight, Tim. Any other progress I should know about?'

'We've identified a couple of suspects for the Gordon murder,' said Pat. 'They're both currently at that farm outside Lyndoch.'

'How do you know that?' said Tim.

'Perhaps I should say their phones are at Lyndoch, and I'm assuming they're attached to them.'

'They have names?' said DCI Roberts.

'Alan Broderick and Edward Handley. Both in their early thirties, and they were at the protest rally with Bragg in December.'

CHAPTER 39

JACK WAS AN EARLY RISER, a habit from his army days that had stayed with him. It was still dark inside the shed when he ventured out of his caravan and made his way to the bathroom on the far side of the building. The silence was absolute, apart from the soft melody of sounds coming from men snoring in their sleeping bags.

As he emerged from the glow of the bathroom lights and re-entered the gloom inside the shed, he felt a vibration in his pocket announcing the arrival of an incoming message. It was 5:04. There was a notification from WhatsApp at the bottom of the screen. The message was from Alf, who was staying with the group at the Tanunda Caravan Park: Police here. Before he could reply, there was a message from another member of the group he knew was in the Nuriootpa Caravan Park: Police here, too!

Boom!

Boom!

Boom!

Jack felt a wave of hot air pushing him backwards. He

fell to the ground. The air filled with smoke. His ears hurt. The smoke stung his throat as he tried to breathe.

'Armed police! Stay where you are!'

There was sound everywhere. The incessant thud, thud, thud of a helicopter directly overhead, so loud it overpowered the sound of voices barking orders. There were bright lights and dogs. Jack felt hands on his shoulders.

'Stay down! Don't move!'

The sound of the helicopter slowly diminished. Thank God, thought Jack. It must be moving away from the immediate area of the shed. The thudding of helicopters was one sound from his army days he could no longer stand.

Jack was led outside, where he was searched, before being ushered onto a waiting bus and handcuffed to the back of a seat. He stared through the bus's smeared windows at what had been their field camp. There were police vehicles everywhere, blue lights flashing, and lines of men being prodded towards the waiting buses where he sat.

Jack leant his head against the glass of the bus window next to his seat. What the fuck had happened?

Margaret was startled awake by a series of loud bangs, followed by the thudding noise made by a helicopter. It was so loud she thought the helicopter had to be on the roof.

After a couple of minutes, the sound of the helicopter subsided and she heard dogs barking and men's voices yelling orders. Then everything went quiet.

She got out of bed and pulled back the curtains. The field of tents next to the shed was visible in the beam of the helicopter's searchlight, although her view was partially blocked by the police car parked in front of her window. It took her a few moments to process what she was looking at, before she understood the place had been raided and she was about to be rescued.

She turned her gaze away from the window at the sound of voices outside her room. The door opened and the room was flooded with a light so bright she had to hold her hands in front of her eyes.

'Don't move!' said a male voice. 'Who are you?'

'Margaret Rutherford.'

The light lost its intensity as the person behind the torch lowered it towards the floor.

'The Chief Magistrate?'

Margaret blinked. She was looking at a police officer wearing a bulletproof vest and holding a pistol. 'Yes.'

'We thought you were dead.'

'So did I,' said Margaret.

'How many other people are there in the house?' said the officer.

'Three.'

The officer holstered his weapon. 'Are you okay?'

'Apart from a sore neck,' said Margaret.

The officer spoke into his radio. 'Sarge, I'm in the back bedroom with the Chief Magistrate.'

There was a commotion outside the door as someone was led down the corridor towards the door that opened onto the back verandah, then a second officer entered the room, a woman with a sergeant's chevron on the front of her vest.

'I'll take it from here, Rick,' said the sergeant, turning on the light at the switch.

The officer with the torch disappeared into the corridor.

'Do you have anything on you to confirm your identity?'

'Jack took my handbag. It'll be in his caravan in the shed, if he still has it.'

'Do you have any clothes? Might not be a good idea to go out there dressed like that.'

Margaret nodded and pointed towards the wardrobe. 'I've got a change of clothes in there.'

'Get dressed. Then, we'll go find your things.'

CHAPTER 40

Saint Ignatius, Norwood, had been Pat's parish church for most of his life, until he'd moved across town to Glenelg following Pam's death. Although he hadn't been inside the building for close on five years, he felt the pull of the familiar atmosphere of his surroundings as he took a seat in the front pew alongside Rose and Alex.

He'd started his education in the school next to the church, before moving on to the senior campus at Athelstone, where he'd met and fallen in love with Pam. Rose and Alex had been baptised in the church and attended the same schools, although they'd lived in Beulah Road, further away from the church than Pat's childhood home.

His parents had lived their entire married life in a house in Gertrude Street, just around the corner from the church, and been faithful members of the parish all that time. Their house was so close they'd walked to church every Sunday morning, right up until the time his mother's arthritis had made that impossible.

Pat's father, Desmond, Des to his friends and family, had left written instructions for his funeral. All he'd wanted was a Requiem Mass. No music, no eulogy, and definitely no PowerPoint presentation of photographs depicting the events of his life. Pat hadn't seen any reason not to grant him that last wish.

The congregation was made up of a smattering of older parishioners, some of whom Pat recognised, his cousins and their children, and a group of Pat's colleagues, including Lina. Des Travers had outlived his siblings and most of his friends.

The stripped-down service took forty-five minutes, during which Pat spent more time wondering about how the morning's raids had gone than listening to the words of the priest.

'Any news?' said Pat, as Lina approached him outside the church.

'All good.'

'This is my son, Alex,' said Pat, remembering his manners. 'Lina Palumbo.'

'Heard a lot about you,' said Alex.

'All good, I hope,' said Lina.

'And, this is Rose,' said Pat, hoping to steer Alex away from divulging too much of what he'd heard.

'Ah, the teacher,' said Lina. 'Don't think I could do what you do.'

Rose smiled. 'It can't be any worse than putting up with Dad.'

'Your father's alright,' said Lina. 'At least he's house trained and does what he's told, most of the time.'

Rose laughed. 'I think she's got your number, Dad.'

'Are you joining us at the Robin Hood?' said Pat.

Lina shook her head. 'Will you be in tomorrow?'

'That's the plan,' said Pat.

'Sorry about your grandfather,' said Lina. 'I'll see you tomorrow, Pat.'

'Thanks for coming.'

As Lina walked towards her car, Rose's husband, Martin, joined them. 'They're ready to go.'

CHAPTER 41

MARGARET WAS RELIEVED to be in her own home after what she'd gone through at the hands of her captors. It felt good to be in her own clothes and in familiar surroundings.

The rope burn mark on her neck had been treated by paramedics at the farm, and she'd been taken to the Royal Adelaide for a battery of tests and a thorough medical examination before she'd been allowed to come home. Fortunately, despite having lost consciousness during her strangulation ordeal, she'd come through the experience with no permanent physical damage. She wasn't so sure she'd come through unscathed psychologically, but she'd have to wait and see how those scars would manifest themselves.

She was sitting at her kitchen table with DCI Roberts, who she'd met on several occasions over the time she'd spent on the bench, and one of his subordinates, DI Ryan, who she assumed was the hands-on lead investigator.

'You know how this works, Your Honour,' said DCI Roberts. 'We're going to need a statement.'

DI Ryan placed his smartphone on the table. 'We'll need

to record this so we can get that statement typed up for you to sign. You okay with that, Your Honour?'

Margaret couldn't help thinking of Vera, one of her favourite TV shows. The detective inspector reminded her of Kenny for some reason. Probably his appearance, if not his smile. 'That's fine, Inspector. Where do you want me to start?'

'Tell us what happened on the night you were abducted? We know you were dropped off around eleven fifteen,' said DI Ryan. 'We've spoken to Randi.'

'He waited until I went into the building. You have to use an access code to open the main entrance. I waved to him once I'd opened the door.' Margaret pictured Randi's smiling face. 'He's such a sweet boy.'

'What happened after you opened the door?'

'I went down the hall to my apartment and opened the door with my key. I switched on the light inside the door and started to disarm the alarm system, only to realise it wasn't on. I was sure I'd turned it on when I was leaving. That's when I saw them. They were standing right next to me.'

'Who was standing next to you?' said DI Ryan.

'Well, I didn't know them from a bar of soap at the time, besides they were wearing face masks. Anyway, the one with the pistol later told me his name was Jack Bragg. He's got a distinctive tattoo on his neck. The other one, I only ever got to learn his first name. Ted.'

DCI Roberts showed her a photograph on his phone. 'This him?'

'Yes.'

'I've just shown the Chief Magistrate a photograph of Edward Handley, also known as Ted Handley.'

'Then what happened?' said DI Ryan.

'They took my handbag, which had my phone in it, and my keys, and led me down to the car park in the basement and forced me into my car. Ted got in the back next to me and put a bag over my head.' Margaret shook her head at the memory of being inside the bag. So claustrophobic. 'Oh, that was dreadful. You have no idea what it's like having a bag over your head. You can't breathe properly, you can't see anything. Anyway, we drove around for quite some time and when they stopped and pulled the bag off, we were inside a shed. I had no idea where I was or what was going to happen to me.'

Margaret closed her eyes and took a deep breath in. She'd been so scared, and talking about it was bringing that feeling back. She let it all flow out with her out breath. She opened her eyes. The policemen were still there, waiting for her to come back to them.

'When did they take the first video?'

'A couple of minutes after we got out of the car. Jack did all the talking. There was another man there who shot the video.'

'Someone besides Ted?'

'Yes, Alan someone.'

'This him?' said DCI Roberts, showing her another photograph on his phone.

'I think so.'

'That's Alan Broderick,' said DCI Roberts.

'What happened after the video shoot?'

'They took me to this room in a corner of the shed. It looked like a prison cell once I was inside it.' Margaret wrapped her arms around herself. 'They told me to take my clothes off. I thought they were going to rape me, but all they wanted was for me to change into an orange boiler suit, like those you see prisoners wearing in American TV shows, and then they locked me in.'

'Did they say anything about what they were doing?'

'Not until breakfast in the morning,' said Margaret. 'We had meals together around a camp kitchen set up in the annex of one of the caravans they had in the shed. It was all very civilised. They told me about their demands. I told them I didn't think they'd get what they wanted. We talked about all sorts of stuff really. They sounded like ordinary blokes, until they started on about being sovereign citizens who were being persecuted by an illegitimate and corrupt state.'

'Did they threaten you at all?'

Margaret shook her head. 'Well, there was the implied threat in the first video, but that relied on them knowing you were hunting them down, but I didn't feel threatened until the others arrived.'

'When was that?'

'People started arriving during the night on Tuesday. There was quite a group for breakfast Wednesday morning.'

'Is that when they carried out the mock execution?'

'That was about an hour after breakfast. I was back in my cell. A bloke wearing a hood came in and handcuffed me with those black plastic tie things. He was rough. Pushed me out into the shed. Said he was carrying out the orders of the court.'

'Do you know who he was?'

'No, I never saw his face. I know it wasn't Jack, though. He was standing behind the camera. I really couldn't see any of their faces, I was looking into the lights they had set up for the filming.'

'Did you see this man at all?' said DCI Roberts, showing

her a photograph that looked like it had been taken for a driver's licence.

'He was at breakfast on Wednesday,' said Margaret. 'Seemed to be someone important. Even Jack was deferential to him. Who is he?'

'That's Alf Martin,' said DCI Roberts. 'He's been identified as the leader of the group.'

'By who?'

DCI Roberts glanced at DI Ryan. 'We're not at liberty to disclose that, Your Honour. Let's just say we have our sources.'

Someone on the inside, thought Margaret. Someone they needed to protect. 'Fair enough.'

'You were found in the farmhouse,' said DI Ryan. 'How did you end up there?'

Margaret shrugged. 'That's where I woke up after I thought I was done for. I've no idea how I got there, but I guess I'd outlived my usefulness as far as the men were concerned.'

'I take it you were still a prisoner,' said DCI Roberts.

'A bit like home detention, I suppose. I was treated more or less as a house guest, like someone staying in a Bed and Breakfast. It's just that there was an armed guard on the garden gate and a field camp full of men across the yard from the house.'

'Who was in the house with you?'

'I was looked after by a young woman who said her name was Erica,' said Margaret, 'and an older couple, Josh and Helen Handley. Erica told me the farm belonged to them and, I don't know if this is important, but Josh has a faded version of the same tattoo as Jack.'

'He's an associate of Jack's father,' said DI Ryan. 'That tattoo has a long history.'

'Is this Erica?' said DCI Roberts, showing her another photograph on his phone.

'Yes. She said she was Jack's partner.'

'That's Erica Bellows,' said DCI Roberts.

Margaret touched her neck. 'She told me this was one of Jack's little jokes.'

'We didn't think it was very funny,' said DI Ryan, 'and I guess he doesn't now either.'

'What will happen to Erica and the Handleys?' said Margaret. 'They were very kind to me.'

'That will depend on how deeply they're involved in this craziness,' said DCI Roberts, 'which we have yet to establish.'

The policemen stood. Margaret understood the interview was over. 'Thank you, gentlemen, and please pass my thanks on to your colleagues. I wasn't sure I was going to live to see today.'

'We're glad you did,' said DCI Roberts. 'We'll be in touch.'

CHAPTER 42

Derek studied Jack Bragg through the two-way mirror. He was sitting in the interview room with his lawyer, Norman Schultz, who had a reputation for providing pro bono defence services for hopeless cases. Derek had heard Norman's services were paid for through crowdfunding. Even sovereign citizens had anonymous benefactors, apparently.

The neck tattoo gave Bragg a menacing appearance but he looked like any other thug to Derek: smug and defiant. Derek wondered how long that would last when the gravity of the situation he'd landed himself in dawned on him.

'Ready, Tim?'

Derek followed Tim Healy into the interview room and sat opposite Jack. He let Tim lead them through the formalities required for the video recording of the interview.

'What are the charges?' said Norman.

'Hasn't he told you?' said Derek.

'I'd like to hear them from you, Inspector.'

Smart-arse, thought Derek. 'Abduction, deprivation of liberty, torture, murder, conspiracy against the State of South

Australia, inciting others to violence. Is that enough to go on, Mr Schultz?'

'That's an interesting list, Inspector. How much of it can you prove?'

'Have you actually spoken to your client, Mr Schultz?'

'My client insists he's innocent of your charges, Inspector.'

'Oh, on what grounds?'

'Jurisprudence, Inspector. A man is innocent until he is proven guilty. You can't just accuse my client of a wrong-doing without evidence.'

'I'm well aware of that, Mr Schultz.' Derek leant back in his seat and looked at Jack Bragg. 'Fortunately, your client has provided us with sufficient evidence for a jury to convict him of several wrongdoings.'

'You're a smug bastard for a copper,' said Jack.

'Oh, I don't think smug is the right word,' said Derek. 'Grateful is what I am. I don't think you appreciate how much of my work you've done for me, Jack. Normally, it would take months to collect the evidence needed to convict someone of the charges you're facing, but, in your case, mate, you handed us the evidence.'

Derek stopped talking and waited. Jack said nothing.

'What did you think we were going to do with your videos?'

'They're just videos,' said Jack.

'They contain some fairly incriminating evidence. Do you want to refresh your memory about what you said and who you filmed?'

'It's just acting,' said Jack. 'It's a joke.'

'A joke? You're telling me you didn't abduct the Chief Magistrate and threaten her life?'

'She's in on it, you moron. Don't you get it?'

'The Chief Magistrate is a sovereign citizen now, is she?'

'Who do you think is in charge of our movement?' Jack smiled. 'She's one of us.'

Derek looked at Norman and raised an eyebrow. 'You do realise we've spoken to the Chief Magistrate and she's told us she was abducted at gunpoint, don't you?'

'She's playing you like the fools you are, mate.'

'Tell me, Jack. How is it you know the Chief Magistrate?'

'She's a friend of my father's.'

'Really? You know we can check that. We could start by asking your father.'

'Go ahead. He met her thirty years ago. Been friends ever since.'

'Funny, she didn't mention that.'

'Did you even ask her?'

Derek smiled. 'I'll ask the questions, Jack.'

'Suit yourself.'

Derek opened his folder and took out a copy of the crime scene report compiled by the investigators who had processed the Chief Magistrate's apartment. 'Care to explain how your fingerprints were found inside the Chief Magistrate's apartment?'

'I was there. She invited me over.'

'On a night she was going to the theatre?'

'We had plans,' said Jack. 'You've seen the video. We had to make it look like she'd been kidnapped to get your attention.' Jack smiled. 'Worked, didn't it?'

'Are you the one who switched off the alarm in her apartment at ten o'clock?'

'Yeah. She sent me the code.'

'As a text message?'

'On WhatsApp,' said Jack. 'You know, it's encrypted, so it's safe.'

'So that would be on her phone, then? And yours?'

'Nah, we deleted it.'

'Are you sure you didn't get that code from this woman?' Derek pushed a photograph of Sally Gordon across the table towards Jack and his lawyer.

'Who's this ugly bitch?'

'Sally Gordon,' said Derek. 'She was the Chief Magistrate's cleaner.'

'Was?' said Norman.

'She's dead,' said Derek. 'Know anything about that, Jack?'

'Nah. I don't need no cleaning woman.'

Derek decided he'd change tack and see where that took them. 'Last Saturday you called Crime Stoppers to tell us where Ella Taylor was. Is that correct?'

'Yeah.'

'Why did you do that?'

'Like I said at the time. A couple of members of our group had gone off the rails with some hare-brained idea for getting the vaccine mandates dropped.'

'Sure it wasn't about getting some of our officers ambushed when they went to investigate?'

'What? I go out of my way to do a community service and you accuse me of sending your officers into an ambush?' Jack turned to Norman. 'See what we're up against?'

'That's a pretty wild accusation, Inspector,' said Norman.

'Want to read the crime scene report, Mr Schultz?' Derek pushed a copy of the report across the table. 'And, we have a statement from someone who was there.'

'Who?' said Jack.

'As I said, Jack. I'll ask the questions.'

They sat in silence while Norman scanned the report.

'How do you know Alf Martin?' said Derek, when Norman had put the crime scene report back on the table.

'We were in the army together.'

'Is that where you met Robbie King and Alan Broderick?'

'You have been doing your homework.'

'What about Ted Handley?'

'Nah, Ted's never been in the army. We've known each other since we were kids. His Dad did things with my old man.'

'We know about some of those things,' said Derek. 'We keep records of our engagements with the public. Guess that's how your Dad met the Chief Magistrate, only she was a magistrate back then.'

'It's not a crime to know someone, mate.'

'Have you worked out how we found out where you were, and what you were planning, Jack?

'We weren't planning anything except a practical joke, you clown.'

'What, with close to a hundred armed men in three camps across the Barossa Valley?'

'We didn't do anything except have a barbecue.'

'Only because we stopped you, Jack. You're lucky someone inside your little band of heroes had second thoughts and spilled the beans before you could stage your act of rebellion. You're lucky no-body got killed, except Sally Gordon, but you'll face a murder charge for that.'

'Says who?' said Jack. 'Your laws don't apply to me!'

'We'll see about that, Jack,' said Derek, 'and, Mr Schultz, we'll be opposing bail.'

'How do you think that went, Tim?'

'Arrogant little prick.'

Derek pulled his papers together and slipped them back into his folder. 'We need to get inside their WhatsApp group.'

'We're working on the phones we've got and that ASIO bloke said they'd send us a copy of the data on their operative's phone.'

'Any idea who he is?'

'They're keeping that close to their chests. I guess he'll have to testify in secret if this goes to trial.'

'Oh, this will go to trial, Tim. These sovereign citizen are clowns and, like all clowns, they love a circus.'

CHAPTER 43

Saturday morning arrived cold and wet, catching Pat unprepared when he stepped outside for his morning walk. He went back inside and found his raincoat before setting out again, determined to stick to his commitment to improve his fitness level and lose weight.

The warm shower felt so much better than it usually did after his walk in the rain. There was something invigorating about venturing out into the elements and surviving. Pat felt ten years younger, even if his body still had some way to go before coming into alignment with that feeling.

By the time he'd showered and dressed, Alex, who was catching the 8:15 flight to Darwin, had left for the airport in a taxi. Despite the circumstances, Pat had enjoyed having his son stay with him and wasn't looking forward to resuming his solo existence. Living alone had its moments, but it could also be lonely.

He thought of Lina. At least he was spending his working hours with someone he liked, and who seemed to enjoy his company as well. Not for the first time, he wished he was twenty years younger and several kilos lighter.

You need to get out more, Travers, he told himself. You're not going to meet someone sitting at home feeling sorry for yourself.

Saturday in the office started with a detailed briefing from Commander O'Loughlin, who'd overseen the STAR Group raids in the Barossa.

Pat listened as the commander told them the raiding parties had detained seventy-six 4 Freedom members, including their leader Alf Martin, and confiscated a hundred and ten weapons along with a considerable amount of ammunition. The commander praised the swift, coordinated action of the raiding parties which, coupled with the element of surprise, had allowed the raids to be concluded without serious injury. He also told them another thirty members of the group had been detained by interstate forces.

The advantage of having inside information, thought Pat. Be great if we had it on every case.

'And, we were relieved to find the Chief Magistrate alive and well,' said Commander O'Loughlin, folding up his notes and turning towards DCI Roberts.

'Yes, she's given us a statement and identified the individuals who abducted her,' said DCI Roberts.

'Well, I'm sure you have plenty to do, Chief Inspector.'

'Thank you, Commander.'

'Over to you, DI Ryan,' said DCI Roberts.

'We've taken initial statements from everyone detained yesterday. Most of them will be bailed, but we'll be opposing bail for the ring leaders and any individuals suspected of being involved in the abduction of the Chief Magistrate and the murder of her cleaner. DS Healy and I have already interviewed Jack Bragg, who seems to think we're a bunch of clowns. He's claiming the Chief Magistrate is in on his little joke, in fact, he's saying she's the leader of the sovereign citizenship movement here in SA.' DI Ryan shook his head. 'He's being defended by Norman Schultz, so that should be interesting.'

A ripple of chuckles moved across the room, confirming for Pat that Norman's reputation was well known across the team.

'DS Travers.'

'Yes, sir,' said Pat.

'I'll leave the interviews of young Handley and Broderick in relation to the Gordon murder in your capable hands.'

Ted Handley had obviously learnt something from his father, thought Pat, as he took his seat in the interview room opposite their suspect.

Handley had declined the services of the duty solicitor and called in his own lawyer, Ross Dunlop, from Dunlop and Furness, who specialised in criminal defence. Pat had first encountered Ross Dunlop when he was a detective constable and knew him as a formidable opponent. He let Lina walk them through the introductions required for the recording.

Pat slid a photograph of Sally Gordon across the table to Ted. 'Do you recognise this woman?'

Ted studied the photograph of a smiling woman in a sundress and looked up at Pat. 'Can't say that I do.'

Pat replaced the photo of Sally in her sundress with one taken by the crime scene investigators who'd examined her house after she'd been killed. 'Perhaps this will jolt your memory.'

Ted sat back quickly in his chair. 'Shit! What happened to her?'

'This woman's name was Sally Gordon. We're investigating her murder. Are you sure you don't recognise her?'

'Got nothing to do with me,' said Ted. 'I've never met her.'

Pat left the photograph on the table in front of Ted, where he couldn't help but see it. 'Ted, do you own a blue Ford Ranger, registration number S379BNH?'

'Yeah.'

'Anyone drive it apart from you?'

'No.'

'So, I can safely assume it was you driving your vehicle when it was photographed by a traffic camera on Greenhill Road last Saturday night?' Pat slid the offending image across the table towards Ted. 'Those numbers across the bottom represent the time and date this photo was taken. The ones at the top are the serial number of the camera at the intersection of Goodwood and Greenhill Roads.'

'Yeah. It's not a crime to drive, is it?'

'Where are you going with this, Sergeant?'

Pat had wondered when Ross would chime in. 'Let me share a few more bits of information with you, Mr Dunlop.'

'I'm all ears, Sergeant.'

'Sally Gordon was the Chief Magistrate's cleaner, Mr Dunlop. She lived in Young Street, Goodwood. I'm sure you're aware by now that your client has been identified by the Chief Magistrate as one of the men who abducted her last Saturday night.' Pat saw the light of understanding dawning in the lawyer's eyes.

'What makes you think my client had anything to do with her murder?'

'Well, we've established he was in the area at the appropriate time,' said Pat. 'In fact, we have a witness that says he saw a blue Ford Ranger parked in front of Sally's house on the evening she was killed, and your client's fingerprints are all over her kitchen.'

'That doesn't mean he killed her.'

'No, but it certainly suggests he was in her house when someone did.'

'I didn't kill her,' said Ted. 'Honest.'

'Do you smoke, Ted?'

'What's that got to do with anything?'

'Yes or no, Ted?'

'No.'

'Does Alan smoke?'

'I don't know. Ask him.'

'I'm asking you, Ted, because he was with you at Sally's place and one of you left a pile of cigarette butts behind.'

Ted dropped his head into his hands.

'We'll have a DNA match for one of you in due course, Ted.'

'It won't be me,' said Ted.

'What happened?'

Ted swallowed, blinking back tears. 'Stupid woman wouldn't hand over the keys, even after I shot her bloody dog.'

'Can we have a break so I can consult with my client, Sergeant?'

Pat looked at his watch and wondered whether he

should push young Handley to a full confession or allow Ross Dunlop to persuade him to make a deal. He knew from his previous dealings with Ross that he would do what was in the best interest of his client, and they'd both heard enough to know what that was. 'Okay, Mr Dunlop. It's nine forty-nine, we'll take a ten-minute break.'

'What do you think he'll do?' said Lina.

'I think he'll spill,' said Pat. 'He's not hardened to killing like some of the others.'

'How do people like Ted get mixed up in this sort of stuff?'

'Someone spins them a yarn and massages their ego, I suppose. It's all great until the shit hits the fan.'

'Bit like joining the force,' said Lina. 'It's all fun until you attend your first domestic or road fatality.'

'Yeah, reality's a bit of a bummer, isn't it?'

Lina looked at him. 'Speaking of reality, how are you coping, Pat? Life hasn't exactly been kind to you recently, has it?'

Pat leant against the wall. 'You expect old people to die, don't you? It's living with the ones that want to hang around I'm worried about.'

'You mean your mother?'

'Can't say I'm looking forward to getting her into an aged care home. She's still insisting she can look after herself.'

'Perhaps we should get my mum to talk to her. She works in aged care.'

'I didn't know that.'

'You never asked.'

'Do you think your mum would do it?'

'We can ask her,' said Lina. 'She's dying to meet you.'

Pat straightened up. 'What have you been telling her?'

Lina laughed. 'Oh, only what a great boss you are.'

After ten minutes they went back into the interview room and resumed their seats. Lina reactivated the video recorder.

'My client wants to strike a plea bargain.'

'What's he offering?'

'He was coerced into taking part in the planned insurrection and the abduction. His parents are in financial strife and he was offered a way out of their problems,' said Ross. 'He's willing to tell you what happened to Ms Gordon in exchange for a non-custodial sentence.'

'That's not much of an exchange,' said Pat. 'We already know what happened to Ms Gordon and pretty soon we'll know who tortured her before she was killed.'

'But you won't know for sure who killed her, will you?'

'I think the DPP is going to want more than that, Mr Dunlop. Is you client willing to tell us all he knows about what Alf Martin and Jack Bragg were planning? Is he willing to testify against them in court?'

'Mr Handley?' said Ross, turning to face his client.

'I don't want to go to gaol,' said Ted. 'I'll tell you everything I know. I'll testify.'

'I'll convey your offer to the Director of Public Prosecutions,' said Pat, 'and we'll take it from there once we know what he's prepared to consider.'

'Thank you,' said Ted.

'Tell me, Ted. How long have you been part of this sovereign citizen movement?'

'Why is that important?'

'Your answer might help the DPP make up his mind about helping you stay out of prison.'

'I've known Jack all my life. Our fathers did things together, things you probably know about.'

'Yes, I was the arresting officer on one of those occasions,' said Pat.

'Really?'

'It's a long story. Tell me about Jack and sovereign citizens.'

'I didn't see him for a few years when he was in the army. He came home about five years ago. That's when he started talking about us being sovereign citizens and the government having no legitimate power over us.'

'When did he start planning this insurrection?'

'Ah, that was Alf's idea. He was in the army with Jack. They've been planning it for years.'

'I think you've got enough of an idea of what my clients has to offer, Sergeant. Give me a call when you've got an answer from the DPP.'

Alan Broderick was escorted into the room with the duty solicitor. Obviously not as well connected as young Ted Handley, thought Pat, as Lina led them through the required opening procedure.

Pat looked at the duty solicitor, who'd introduced herself as Miriam Wales. He hadn't come across her before and thought she must be new to the panel. However, the way in which she'd presented herself to them made him think she wasn't a recent addition to the legal profession, and neither was she someone to be trifled with.

'Have you been briefed on the charges Mr Broderick is facing, Ms Wales?'

'I understand this is in addition to the charges connected to the alleged insurrection and abduction, Sergeant, which, by the way, my client is denying.'

Pat knew from what Tim Healy had told him that Broderick had played the sovereign citizen card during their interview, and wondered how long he'd wait before raising it again. 'Where were you around seven o'clock last Saturday evening, Alan?'

'What's it to you?'

'That's not an appropriate answer, Mr Broderick,' said Miriam. 'Either answer the question or say no comment if you don't want to answer the question. This is not a game of bad manners.'

Broderick straightened in his chair. 'No comment.'

Miriam Wales was obviously old school, a stickler for civil behaviour, thought Pat, as he took a sheet of paper out of his folder and slid it across the table so Alan could read it. 'This is a printout of the location data for your mobile phone. It shows us where it and presumably you were last Saturday night, since you were relieved of your phone yesterday.' Pat pointed to a line he'd highlighted with a yellow marker pen. 'This places you in the vicinity of Young Street, Goodwood, for at least forty minutes, starting at three minutes past seven.'

Alan stared at Pat and shrugged.

Pat moved the sheet of paper into the reach of Miriam and waited for her to read the details.

'Why is this important, Sergeant?'

'Young Street is where this woman lived.' He took the photograph of Sally Gordon in her sundress out of his folder and showed it to Alan. 'Remember her, Alan?'

'No comment.'

'In the next day or two, Alan, we'll have the results from comparing your DNA with the profile of the person who left a pile of cigarette butts in her house after she'd been tortured and murdered.' Pat looked at Alan. 'Do you smoke?'

'No comment.'

'We know Ted was there with you, Alan. He left his fingerprints all over the place but, as I'm sure you know, he doesn't smoke.'

'You know you have no jurisdiction over me, don't you?'

Here it comes, thought Pat. 'Says who?'

'Me! I haven't agreed to live by your rules. You can't keep me here!'

Miriam rolled her eyes. She'd obviously heard Alan's sovereign citizen spiel before. Pat wondered if she'd intervene again or let Broderick hang himself. She rested her hands in her lap and smiled at him. Pat took that as a signal that she was going to sit this round out and see how he handled it.

Pat glanced at Lina. Her face was poker straight, but he saw the twinkle in her eye that told him she was waiting to see how he handled Broderick's bullshit as well. He turned his attention back to the man sitting across the table from him. 'If you don't want to live by our rules, as you call them, why are you in our country? You know you can always leave and go live in a country with laws more to your liking.'

'Don't try and be a smart-arse, copper. I know my rights!'

'Is that going to be your defence to a murder charge?'

'I don't need a defence, mate. I haven't killed anyone!'

Pat gathered his papers and put them back into his folder. 'Alan, in addition to the other charges you're facing, we're holding you on suspicion of being responsible for the murder of Sally Gordon. We know you were in the vicinity, your phone records prove that, and we have a credible witness who claims you killed her.' Pat folded his arms.

'You're wasting your time, mate. I'll be suing you for wrongful arrest!'

'Didn't think you respected the power of our courts, Alan.'

'Too bloody right I don't!'

Pat smiled. Broderick obviously didn't see the inconsistency in his argument. 'Interview terminated. We'll speak again, Mr Broderick, when we have those DNA results.'

CHAPTER 44

DEREK READ through his notes while they waited for Alf Martin and his lawyer. ASIO had supplied them with a concise background briefing on Martin. He was forty-three, had served as an officer in the Special Air Services Regiment, doing two tours of Afghanistan, where he'd commanded several of the men he'd recruited into 4 Freedom, including Bragg and Broderick, before he took a voluntary discharge in 2014 and returned to Ballarat, Victoria, where he'd lived before enlisting.

Divorced, Martin was estranged from his teenage children. He operated a business specialising in mountain bikes in Ballarat, and had come to the attention of ASIO when he'd started recruiting veterans to participate in anti-government protests.

The door opened. Alf Martin, wearing the clothes he'd been arrested in, and a man, in a dark grey suit with matching tie on a white shirt, were ushered into the interview room.

'George Willis,' said the lawyer. 'Mr Martin has engaged me to represent his interests.'

'Have a seat,' said Derek, wondering where Martin had found this pompous prick at such short notice. 'Let's get this show on the road, Sergeant.'

Derek studied Alf Martin's face while DS Healy got the proceedings underway. The man was giving nothing away. Derek wondered if Martin had any idea how draconian the anti-terrorism laws were or if he knew he'd be talking to the AFP after Derek had finished with him.

'Care to explain why you were in the Tanunda Caravan Park yesterday, Mr Martin?'

'I was visiting your famous Barossa Valley, Inspector.' Alf smiled. 'I don't mind a good red. I hear they make fine wine up there.'

'You're saying you're here as a tourist?'

'Yes, Inspector. I'm over here helping your tourism industry get back on its feet after the pandemic.'

'That's mighty generous of you, Mr Martin. Is that why you were with a party of twelve staying in cabins in the caravan park?'

'We're on a wine tour, Inspector. Surely you've heard of group bookings?'

'Yes, I've been on a few myself,' said Derek, 'but not with mates armed to the teeth with unregistered firearms.'

'How was I to know they were unregistered, Inspector?' Alf shrugged. 'We're going up north hunting feral pigs after the Barossa tour and, as I'm sure you're aware, my rifle is registered.'

Derek looked down at his notes, as if he was checking something. 'I understand you travelled to Adelaide separately, Mr Martin. The location data from your phone has you in Semaphore last Saturday, in the vicinity of Jack Bragg's address.'

'Jack served with me in Afghanistan, Inspector. We were catching up. He's been planning a get together for veterans for some time. A lot of guys come out of the services with issues.' Alf looked Derek in the eyes. 'He was trying to do something for them, but you lot have stuffed that, haven't you?'

At least he's sticking to the same script, thought Derek, who'd read through the statements made by the men detained alongside Martin before starting the interview. 'There's only one thing wrong with your story, Mr Martin. It's not true.'

'Your word against mine, Inspector.'

'It doesn't actually work that way, Mr Martin. The courts usually want to see some evidence backing up my story, at least. Of course, you're free to spin any yarn you choose but, as I'm sure Mr Willis will tell you, we're free to challenge your version of events, and the court will require corroboratory evidence to back up your story.'

'You've got nothing on me, Inspector. You can't even ping me for having an unregistered firearm.'

'It's not your firearm that's your problem, Mr Martin. It's your phone.'

'What are you talking about? Phones don't have to be registered.'

'But, in a way, they are, aren't they?'

Alf leant back in his chair. 'So, you can track my movements. So what? I haven't been anywhere illegal.'

'Your group, what do you call yourselves? 4 Freedom. Is that it?'

'Well, that's what we stand for. Freedom.'

'You communicate among yourselves using WhatsApp, don't you?'

'Yes, it's encrypted so people like you can't listen in. What's wrong with that? Lots of people use it.'

'Nothing wrong with it. I use it myself, but group chats have a vulnerability, Mr Martin. The more members, the greater the chance of a leak.'

Alf crossed his arms. 'That's only a problem if you're doing something illegal, Inspector. Organising protests, isn't illegal, especially when you've obtained authorisation. And organising a tour of the Barossa certainly isn't illegal.'

'But organising an insurrection, or planning an abduction or two, or perhaps planning an ambush of police, would you say that was illegal?'

'Sounds like it to me, Inspector. Just as well I haven't been doing any of those things.'

Smug bastard, thought Derek. He has no idea his inner circle has been infiltrated. 'You heard of ASIO, Mr Martin?'

'Who hasn't?'

'Well, they've heard of you, Mr Martin, and taken a keen interest in your activities. In fact, they've got someone in your WhatsApp Planning Group.'

The colour drained from Alf's face. He'd obviously realised the implication of Derek's revelation. 'The Federal Police handle terrorism cases, Mr Martin, and we'll be handing you over to them once we've sorted out your involvement in the planning and execution of crimes covered in this jurisdiction.'

'What crimes?' said Alf. 'I haven't committed any crimes.'

'There's the abduction of Ella Taylor and the death of her mother, and then there's the abduction and torture of the Chief Magistrate, and the death of her cleaner.'

'I had nothing to do with any of that.'

'Conspiracy to commit, or planning if you'd prefer that word, is a crime, Mr Martin, even if you don't actually carry out the criminal actions planned yourself.'

Alf turned to his lawyer.

'What evidence do you have for these wild allegations, Inspector?'

'We can provide you with a copy of the relevant transcripts of your client's planning group conversations, along with a list of identifying phone numbers, Mr Willis. I'm sure the AFP will fill you in on the other parts.'

'My client will not be answering any more of your questions, Inspector.'

'That's his prerogative,' said Derek, 'but we'll be opposing bail when he comes before the magistrate on those conspiracy charges I mentioned.'

'Your courts have no legitimate jurisdiction,' said Alf.

'Not now, Mr Martin,' said George. 'The inspector is a policeman, not a magistrate. We can have that argument in court.'

CHAPTER 45

ALAN BRODERICK STOPPED TALKING to his lawyer as soon as Pat and Lina entered the interview room and activated the recording equipment.

'We have the results from the tests we ran on your DNA, Alan. They confirm you were the person who smoked the cigarettes left at the scene of Sally Gordon's torture and execution.'

'All that means is I was in her house,' said Alan. 'Nothing else. In fact, it could mean someone planted a pile of cigarette butts I'd discarded some place else. You've got nothing, copper!'

Pat looked at Miriam Wales, who Broderick had retained for his defence.

'He's got a point, Sergeant.'

'Not when we match this with the location data from his phone. When we put those two sets of data together we have your client in the victim's house at the time she was killed, in the very room where her body was found tied to a chair,' said Pat. 'And, let's not forget, Ted Handley has confessed to being there watching, while Alan tortured Sally Gordon and then strangled her once she'd told them what they wanted to know.'

'That little shit would say anything to save his own neck!'

'And you, being a man of honour, wouldn't? Whose leg do you think you're pulling, Alan?' Pat took a couple of deep breaths, aware he needed to stay in control of his emotions. 'Young Handley may have shot her dog, but I don't think he's got what it takes to kill another human being. But someone with your training and battlefield experience.' Pat paused for effect. He wanted Broderick to know he was under no illusions as to his guilt. 'That's a different story, isn't it?'

'No comment.'

'Want to talk us through what happened on the night you went to Sally Gordon's house with Ted?'

'No comment.'

'Suit yourself,' said Pat, turning to Miriam. 'I'll see you get a copy of Ted's statement in due course.'

'Thank you, Sergeant.'

'You're being charged with murder,' said Pat. 'Do you understand the charge, Alan?'

'Charge me with whatever you like, copper. Doesn't make any difference to me.' Broderick sat back in his chair. 'It's all bullshit!'

———

'That went well,' said Lina, as they walked across the Remand Centre car park towards their car.

'At least he didn't get on his soap box about being a sovereign citizen again.'

'I think his lawyer might have knocked that out of him.

She doesn't strike me as someone who'd put up with that sort of shit.'

'Well, let's hope she can talk him into pleading guilty before this goes to trial,' said Pat. 'That'll make life easier for us.'

'We're still going to have to write this up, though, just in case he doesn't.'

'I guess that's life,' said Pat. 'Come on, I'll buy you a coffee before we head back.'

CHAPTER 46

TESSA OPENED the back door to the farmhouse and ushered Mia through the mudroom into the kitchen.

'Mummy, what's that funny smell?'

The house, which had been closed up since the day the police had arrested Robbie and Jordan and confiscated the guns they'd planned to use in the ambush, appeared to be in order, despite Tessa's worst fears about the mess a search would leave behind. The rank odour filling the kitchen, however, told her none of the officers who'd searched the house had had the presence of mind to empty the scraps bucket in the cupboard under the sink.

'Let me open the window,' said Tessa, dumping her bag of groceries on the kitchen table and crossing to the window, before taking the offending bucket of rotting food scraps outside.

Mia followed her into the garden. 'When's daddy coming home?'

Tessa emptied the bucket onto the compost heap and squatted to be at eye level with Mia. 'Daddy's not coming home, sweetheart. It's going to be just you and me now.'

Mia bit her bottom lip. 'Is Uncle Jordan coming home?'

'Not for a very long time.'

Mia put her hands on her hips. 'Who's going to feed the chooks?'

Shit, thought Tessa, standing up to her full height, wondering if anyone had fed them while they'd been away. She hadn't thought to ring any of the neighbours to ask them to keep an eye on the place. She was suddenly aware of the possibility that if none of the neighbours had stepped in voluntarily to feed them, the hens would be dead and there wouldn't be any fresh eggs.

'Guess we'd better go and see if the chooks are still here,' said Tessa, wondering if what she was suggesting was a good idea, while at the same time knowing she'd have to explain to Mia at some point if the hens had perished while they'd been in protective custody. 'Go in and get the egg basket from the laundry.'

They crossed the yard to the implement shed, Mia skipping along ahead of Tessa with the egg basket swinging in her left hand. As they entered the shed and walked towards the door in the back wall that opened into the chicken run, Tessa was relieved to hear the sound of clucking. Thank God, someone had thought to feed the hens. She opened the hatch to allow Mia to collect the eggs. Thankfully, there appeared to be only a day's supply of eggs, telling her whoever had fed the hens had also been collecting their eggs.

While Mia gathered the eggs, Tessa went into the henhouse to check on their water and top up the feeder with grain. Looking after the hens had been one of her childhood chores and being with them had always made her feel safe. She was grateful someone had thought to look after them and hoped she'd find out who that had been.

As they headed back across the yard with their basket of eggs, a small white car rolled to a stop in the yard and a young man, who Tessa recognised as one of the policemen she'd spoken to at Mt Barker, climbed out of it.

'Ah, you're back.'

'We got back today,' said Tessa, wondering what he wanted. 'What are you doing here? Is there something wrong?'

'I'm sorry. I didn't mean to startle you. My parents' place is just up the road. My mum was worried about your chooks.' He smiled. 'I've been dropping in to feed them on my way home from work.'

'Thank you,' said Tessa. 'I must admit, I forgot all about them.'

'Better thank my mum. It was her idea.'

'What was your name again?' said Tessa.

'Andrew. Andrew Rodgers. You spoke to me when you came to the station in Mt Barker.' He smiled.

Tessa liked his smile. 'Oh, that's right. Can I offer you a coffee, Andrew?'

He glanced at Mia and Tessa thought he was about to decline her offer.

'Sure. Why not?'

Tessa was glad she'd opened the kitchen window before they'd ventured into the henhouse, as the foul odour that had greeted them when she'd first entered the house had dissipated by the time they returned with Andrew. Tessa got Mia a drink and a snack and sent her into watch something on the kids channel.

'Sorry about the mess, but we'd only just got home when Mia reminded me about the chooks.'

Andrew glanced around the kitchen. 'Doesn't look any worse than our place. Mum's always got things everywhere.'

Tessa thought he was old enough to have found a place of his own and wondered if he was younger than he looked. She'd assumed from his appearance that he was about her age. 'You living at home, then?'

'Yeah. Dad's got a few health issues, so I've moved back in to help run the farm until he gets better.'

That made more sense, thought Tessa. 'Does that interfere with your work?'

'I'm working around it and it won't be forever, unless I decide to take over the farm. What are you going to do about this place?'

Tessa filled the kettle and switched it on, thinking Andrew sounded more like a farmer's son than a policeman. 'I'll have to do something. My brother isn't going to be around for a while. What do you think he'll get for kidnapping?'

'Is he pleading guilty?'

'Pretty hard for him not to given what I've told you lot.'

'Ten to fifteen at a guess. Will depend on the judge, of course. What's your husband being charged with?'

'He's pleading guilty to kidnapping and manslaughter.'

'Can't see him getting out for at least twenty years.'

'Serves him bloody right,' said Tessa. 'I won't be waiting around for him or visiting him anytime soon.'

'Can't say I blame you. So, are you going to run the place or sell it?'

'I can hardly sell it. It belongs to Jordan. Won't ever be mine unless he dies before I do.' Tessa shook her head. 'And, there I was, getting him arrested to save his life.' She laughed. 'Anyway, he told me, through his lawyer, mind you, to get someone to help me run the place.' She smiled at Andrew. 'Suggested your father, in fact. Said he was an honest bloke.'

'He's honest all right but it will be a couple of months before he's back in the saddle, and you're going to need help organising the apple harvest before then.'

Tessa made their coffees and they sat at the kitchen table. 'Do you know anyone I could talk to?'

'Let me talk to the contractor we use,' said Andrew. 'I'm surprised your brother hasn't got someone lined up.'

Tessa shrugged. 'He thought we'd all be dead, so he didn't bother arranging anything for this year's harvest.'

Andrew took a sip of his coffee. 'Well, I'm glad he got that wrong.'

'Me too,' said Tessa. 'He was planning on shooting people like you, and if he'd done that, who would have looked after the chooks?'

'And, if you don't mind me asking, Tessa. What's going to happen to you?'

'They're not charging me in exchange for freeing Ella and telling them what I knew, given what I'd been subjected to.'

Andrew nodded. 'Well that's good. At least you'll be able to look after Mia.'

'Yeah, and get away from Robbie. You have no idea what he put me through.'

'If you ever want to talk about it, I'm a good listener.'

'Maybe another time,' said Tessa, hoping he'd come back and spend more time with her. She felt safe with Andrew. He had a calming energy about him and she wondered why she couldn't recall him from her childhood, since the

Rodgers' farm was one of the neighbouring properties. 'We're about the same age, Andrew, how come I don't remember you from school?'

'I went to Cornerstone, in Mt Barker.'

'Oh, that would explain it. We went to Oakbank Area.'

'I won't hold that against you,' said Andrew, placing his empty mug on the table. 'I'll have a word with my dad and our contractor and see what we can work out for you about harvest time. Be a pity to see all those apples go to waste.'

'Thanks.'

'I'll be in touch when I've got some news.'

'Drop in anytime, Andrew. And, thanks for looking after the chooks.'

Tessa walked him to his car, and watched him drive up the driveway towards the road before heading back inside to check on Mia. She hoped it wouldn't be too long before she saw him again.

CHAPTER 47

PAT ARRIVED at the address in Lockleys that Lina had given him right on six-thirty, relieved to see her car in the driveway. It was a modest sized house with a Basket Range Sandstone facade, a style which had been popular in the 1960s. He parked behind the white BMW sedan standing in the street in front of the house, retrieved the bottle of white wine he'd been instructed to bring from the insulated wine bag he'd stowed behind his seat, and made his way to the front door.

As he waited to be admitted, he hoped he'd made the right decision agreeing to meet with Lina's mother in her home, instead of in a Henley Square coffee shop where he'd feel more relaxed. But, he'd lost that argument when Lina had explained that cooking a meal for him was her mother's way of doing things. She was Italian, after all, and eating together was a cultural thing. At least, that's how Lina had sold it to him.

The door opened. Lina smiled at him. She was wearing a sleeveless soft-yellow frock, strikingly different to the business suits she wore to work. Pat hoped his jaw hadn't dropped.

'Hi, Pat!'

Pat stepped back. 'Almost didn't recognise you.'

Lina laughed. 'Well, this is me at home. Do you like it?'

'Very nice,' said Pat.

'Let me take that bottle for you', said Lina, as she ushered him in and closed the door. 'The others are through there.'

Others? Pat wondered who else had been invited, since Lina had told him her father had gone fishing with his mates for the weekend.

He followed Lina into the dining room. The table was set for four. She led him into the kitchen, where two women, who Pat decided had to be sisters, were putting the finishing touches to what would be their evening meal.

'Ma, this is Pat.'

'Call me Rita,' said the woman with greying hair, shaking Pat's hand. 'This is my sister, Angela.'

'Pleased to meet you,' said Pat.

'Angela Romeo,' said the woman with hair as dark as Lina's, taking his hand in hers. 'Hope you're hungry.'

Pat looked at the plates of steaming pasta marinara and the bowls of salad waiting to be carried into the dining room. He'd have to exercise restraint if he didn't want to starve himself for the next couple of days. 'Look's delicious.'

'It's okay, Pat. You don't have to eat it all,' said Rita, smiling. 'I won't be offended.'

'It will be hard to resist this,' said Pat, pointing at the food.

'Shall we eat?' said Angela, lifting two plates of pasta off the bench. 'I'm starving!'

Pat found himself seated opposite Rita, next to Angela. Lina poured them each a glass of wine and they spent several minutes eating. Pasta marinara was one of Pat's favourite Italian dishes and he concentrated on not splashing bits of the marinara sauce over the white tablecloth as he was forking it into his mouth.

'That was delicious,' said Pat.

'Would you like another plate?' said Rita.

Pat was tempted but declined the offer of a second helping of pasta. He'd seen the covered plate piled with crumbed veal cutlets on the table next to the bowls of salad, and Lina had warned him her mother was making apple pie for dessert.

When they'd finished with the pasta marinara, Lina cleared the pasta plates from the table and they helped them-selves to the crumbed veal and salads.

'How long have you been a policeman?' said Angela.

'Bit over thirty years,' said Pat, feeling at ease in her company. 'What do you do with yourself?'

'I'm an accountant,' said Angela, 'like my sister.'

Pat turned to Rita. 'I thought you worked in aged care?'

'Were you expecting me to be a carer or a nurse?' said Rita, laughing. 'Didn't Lina tell you I was in administration?'

'No, I think she might have skipped that detail, not that it matters.' Pat looked at Lina. Her face told him something beyond the obvious was going on, something he couldn't quite put his finger on.

'It means I can give your mother an overview of the facil-ities we offer and arrange a tour for her,' said Rita. 'It also means I'll know when something suitable becomes available for her to move into.'

'They're doing her assessment this week,' said Pat, telling himself to stop reading things into Lina's expression.

'What day?'

'Wednesday.'

'Perhaps we can make a time to talk to her after that,' said Rita. 'I'm free most nights after six.'

'That would be good,' said Pat. 'How about Thursday? I could drop by and pick you up. She's still out at Hampstead.'

Rita looked at the calendar on her phone. 'I could meet your there at, let's see, six-thirty? I'll be at one of our homes on that side of town this Thursday.'

'Okay.' Pat entered the details into his calendar and gave Rita the address of the ward his mother was recuperating in.

'How is your mother?' said Rita.

'Injury wise, she's making good progress according to the doctors. Attitude wise, it's a bit of a different story. She's still insisting she can manage by herself at home, despite her mobility issues and her arthritis.'

'That's not uncommon,' said Rita. 'It's a big decision giving up your independence and moving into an aged care unit.'

'I don't think she'll have much choice,' said Pat.

'It's okay, Pat. We'll find a way,' said Rita. 'I've helped lots of people like your mother make the transition.'

'Thanks,' said Pat, wondering what he'd done to deserve her help.

They spent the next few minutes eating veal cutlets and salad.

'So, Angela, do you work for yourself or are you in administration like Rita?' said Pat, pushing his empty plate towards the middle of the table.

'I'm in partnership with my brother-in-law,' said Angela. 'He bought into the practice when my husband died.'

'Oh, I'm sorry to hear that,' said Pat. 'How long ago?'

'Four years, last Christmas.'

'Accident or illness?'

'Accident,' said Angela. 'He was knocked off his bike on Portrush Road.'

'I think that's worse than dying from an illness,' said Pat. 'At least when my wife was dying of breast cancer we knew it was happening.'

'Lina says you have children. How did they take it?'

'My kids are grown up. They left home years before Pam died. I think Rose, my daughter, found it the hardest. Breast cancer hits a bit closer to home for a daughter.'

Angela nodded. 'Mine are in their early twenties. I'm not sure they're over the shock of it.'

'And, what about you?'

'It was hard in the early days. I still think of him all the time, but I'm starting to think it's time to move on.' Angela threw her head back and smiled. She had that same smile he found so endearing in Lina. 'I'm still young. I've got a life to live.'

'Yeah, I've been thinking about that too.'

'Is that why you're working out, Pat?' said Lina, placing a piece of apple pie smothered in cream in front of him. 'Getting back in shape to impress the girls?'

'Thought had crossed my mind,' said Pat. 'Is it working?'

'Not with me,' said Lina, laughing. 'I'm not into older men.'

'You don't look beyond redemption, Pat' said Angela. 'Maybe all you need is a woman's touch in your life.'

'Yeah, you should see his work clothes,' said Lina.

'I have a few clients in the fashion industry. Perhaps I should take you shopping so you can brush up your professional image.'

There was that smile again. Pat could feel a warmth spreading across his cheeks. 'I might take you up on that.'

'Might?' said Angela. 'I'll have you know, Pat Travers, I don't make these offers to every Tom, Dick or Harry.'

'Then I'm flattered,' said Pat. 'I've got this week off. When could you fit me in?'

'How about tomorrow?' said Angela. 'I could meet you in Hyde Park at ten. I've got a client with a menswear store on King William Road. Perhaps we could do lunch afterwards.'

That sounded good to Pat. 'Okay, let's do it.' He took out his phone, opened the calendar app, keyed in the details, and then exchanged numbers with Angela.

'Coffee, anyone?' said Rita, coming in from the kitchen.

'Yes, thank you,' said Pat, wondering what had just happened to him. He looked at Lina. She flashed a smile at him from across the table, a smile that gradually took on a new meaning as it dawned on him what she'd done. She'd taken advantage of the dinner to arranged the encounter with Angela, knowing they both needed someone new in their lives.

He didn't know how she'd known they would hit it off, but was grateful she had, and felt excited at the prospect of finding out if Monday's shopping trip would lead to anything beyond lunch with Angela.

A NOTE FROM PETER

If you enjoyed *Distraction,* you can help other readers share your enjoyment by telling them about the book and writing a review.

Drop by at **www.petermulraney.com** and join my **Crime Readers Group** to download a free copy of *Deadly Sands,* and be one of the first to know when my next book will be released.

ALSO BY PETER MULRANEY

Travers and Palumbo series

Desolation

Inspector West series

After

The Holiday

Holy Death

Whistleblower

Twisted Justice

The East Park Syndicate

Inspector West Collection One

Inspector West Collection Two

Stella Bruno Investigates series

The Identity Thief

A Gun of Many Parts

Bones in the Forest

A Deadly Game of Hangman

Taken

Fallout

The Melrose Case

The Scam

Deception

Stella Bruno Investigates: Books 1 to 6

The Identity Thief Collection

The Fallout Collection

The Deception Collection

Ryan Holiday PI Short Stories

Rosie

Framed

Novella

The New Girlfriend

Living Alone series

After She's Gone

Cooking 4 One

Sanity Savers

Living Alone (Collection)

Living Alone Journal

Everyday Business Skills

Everyday Project Management

Everyday Productivity

Everyday Money Management

Writings of the Mystic

Sharing the Journey: Reflections of a Reluctant Mystic

My Life is My Responsibility: Insights for Conscious Living

I Am Affirmations: The Power of Words

Beyond the Words: Reflections on I Am Affirmations

Mystical Journey: A Handbook for Modern Mystics

Sharing the Journey Coloring Books

Mandalas

Mandalas by 3

Sharing the Journey Coloring Journals

Sharing the Journey Coloring Journal

Sharing the Journey Coloring Journal ~Discovery

Sharing the Journey Coloring Journal ~ Reflection

www.ingramcontent.com/pod-product-compliance
Lightning Source LLC
Chambersburg PA
CBHW020508120726
47904CB00003B/752